Sweet William

Sweet William

A NOVEL BY

Beryl Bainbridge

GEORGE BRAZILLER   *New York*

Published in the United States in 1976 by George Braziller,
Inc.
Copyright © 1975 by Beryl Bainbridge
Originally published in London by Gerald Duckworth & Co.
Ltd.

Library of Congress Cataloging in Publication Data
Bainbridge, Beryl, 1933–
 Sweet William.

 I. Title.
PZ4.B162Sw4 [PR6052.A3195] 823'.9'14 75–43672
ISBN 0–8076–0816–5

Printed in the United States of America
First Printing, February, 1976
Second Printing, March, 1976

for Jimmy Boots

1

In the main entrance of the air terminal a young man stood beside a cigarette machine, searching in the breast pocket of his blue suit for his passport. A girl, slouching in a grey coat, as if she thought she was too tall, passively watched him.

"It's safe," he said, patting his jacket with relief.

Suddenly the girl's face, reflected in the chrome surface of the tobacco machine, changed expression. Clownishly her mouth turned down at the corners.

"You should have taken me with you," she said. "You should have done."

He knew she was right, and yet how could he arrive in the States with someone who was not his wife? It wasn't like London. The University would never stand for him living with a woman, not in quarters provided and paid for by the faculty.

"I'll send for you," he told her. "I'll send for you very soon."

She thought how handsome he was, with his dark hair cut short to impress his transatlantic colleagues, his chelsea boots. There hadn't been time for him to put on a tie, and his shirt was unbuttoned at the neck. It occurred to her how masculine he was and how unfair that she should realise it only when saying goodbye.

"Jesus," he said. "Look at the clock. I'll have to move, Ann."

"Wait," she pleaded. And he looked desperately at the queue forming outside the door leading to the coach park. "All right," she said bitterly. "Go."

He bent to pick up his suitcase and his white raincoat. She stood turned away from him with a bright deliberate smile on her face. He put down his case and touched her arm.

He said uneasily, "I'll miss the plane."

She relented and allowed him to embrace her. When they kissed, she felt her stomach turn over; it was probably the excitement of losing him. When they had been together she always stood outside, observing them both.

He didn't turn round to wave as he went through the departure door, nor did she follow to watch him boarding the coach. Acting out the fantasy that she had been betrayed, she stumbled with bowed head towards the exit. She was already feeling a little frightened at the thought of facing her mother. Maybe if she bought some fresh rolls on the Finchley Road and a bunch of flowers for her breakfast tray, Mrs. Walton would be less condemning. She might even be sympathetic; after all, it had been her idea that Ann get engaged. Ann hadn't thought she knew Gerald well enough—they had only known each other for a few weeks when he was offered the University post—but Mrs. Walton said she would be a fool to think it over, particularly as Gerald was flying off to America and with such splendid prospects. She hadn't met Gerald then, but her friend Mrs. Munro, with whom she played bridge, had a daughter married to an American, and Mrs. Munro had made three trips to the States in four years.

When the No. 13 bus came, Ann sat on the top deck at the front holding tightly to the chrome rail as the vehicle tore between the parked cars and the tattered trees. She closed her eyes and relived Gerald kissing her goodbye. The excitement was still there—the sensation in the pit of her stomach—though she couldn't be sure it wasn't panic at the thought of the scene to come. Mrs. Walton had insisted on travelling up from Brighton to be introduced to Gerald before he departed. It was natural enough that she should want to meet him, though she could have chosen a more convenient time. She'd brought a large suitcase too, as if it was going to be a lengthy visit, although she knew Pamela was arriving the day after tomorrow and there wasn't room for them all; there weren't enough sheets or blankets. Ann had asked her mother to come ten days ago but Mrs. Walton said she hadn't a spare moment. She had a busy agenda; there was a bridge evening arranged. The night before, Gerald's friends had given him a farewell party to which Mrs. Walton wasn't invited. "Don't be ridiculous," snapped Gerald when Ann hinted that perhaps they should take Mrs. Walton. "You can't take your mother with you." Mrs. Walton's mouth trembled the way it always did when she was put out about something. "I had thought," she said, "that we'd stay in and perhaps have a nice round of cards." And Gerald said "Tough" under his breath. But she heard. Ann worried all evening about her mother being upset, and Gerald drank too much. When he brought her home he pushed his way into the flat and tried to make her take her clothes off. She wouldn't remove all of them, in case her mother came out of the bedroom. He bent her over the sofa and made love to her standing up. It didn't work very well because he was too drunk; every time he lunged forward she was pressed against the upholstered arm, and dust filled her nose. They couldn't lie down because the floor creaked. Gerald became terribly irritated by her lack of cooperation, but there was nothing she could do. Mrs. Walton started moving about in the other room and coughing and calling out for cups of water. In the end Gerald swore and made a dreadful noise going downstairs—a sort of howl like a dog on the end of a chain. It was astonishing Mrs. Walton didn't come out in her white nylon nightgown and confront them both. She wasn't a coward.

The bus circled the roundabout and Ann looked down on Lords Cricket Ground. There was a man in a boy's cap running towards the fence. He flung his arm high into the air as if he was going to do a hand stand on the green grass. A van with a sprinkler advanced along the perimeter of the field, and the bowler plodded, bandy-legged and perspiring, back to his starting point. Ann couldn't think what

10

to say to her mother. She'd have to play it by ear—keep a straight bat and hope she wasn't caught leg before wicket. Silly mid-off, she thought, and tore her bus ticket into little pieces.

She bought the rolls and six carnations, and some fresh eggs from the health food shop. There probably wasn't any difference between those and the ones in the supermarket, but she felt she was being nice to her mother—filling her up with goodness, nothing but the best. She made a lot of noise going up the stairs, thumping her feet at every step to give Mrs. Walton time to put back any correspondence she might have found in the flat. She didn't mind the way her mother spied on her, the detective work she felt compelled to do; there wasn't anything sensational to find, and her father was such a private man her mother had a need to discover secrets.

However, her mother was packing.

"What are you doing?" asked Ann, though it was obvious.

"I'm leaving," said Mrs. Walton. She had been crying, and she wore her bedjacket, the one with the blue ribbons. She looked like an overfed baby with her flushed cheeks, her diminutive mouth, and the little plump arms appearing from the beribboned sleeves of the fluffy bedjacket.

"Oh," said Ann. "I thought you might stay to see Pamela."

"I know when I'm not wanted," said Mrs. Walton, though she had never known.

Ann realised it was too late to pretend innocence; she had to attack. "I can't understand you," she cried fiercely. "You said you wanted to meet Gerald

11

and yet you hardly spoke to him. He thought it was odd."

"Don't talk to me," said Mrs. Walton, pushing a blue taffeta dress into the suitcase.

Ann watched her in silence for a moment. "I bought you some flowers." She laid the carnations on the coverlet.

"I did not come here," her mother explained, "to put up with you running all over London with that person, and carrying on half the night."

"That person," said Ann, feeling on safer ground, "is the one you told me to get engaged to. He's going to be your son-in-law."

Mrs. Walton made a contemptuous sound. Her eyes registered disbelief.

"Never," she said. "Not after last night. You and him . . . the noises . . . the grunting."

It did seem disgusting the way she described it. Ann remembered a holiday she had spent as a child on a farm in Wiltshire. Four days, bed and break-fast, and the rain sloping down across the fields. Her mother, in gum boots and headscarf, took her to see the cows in their shed. The animals coughed in the dark stalls and rattled their chains. "Look darling," cried Mrs. Walton, wrinkling her sensitive nose at the smell of the dung, "Aren't they sweet?" At the end of the cobbled yard was a sty. They could hear the sounds of slaughter as they came out of the cow shed. "Wait," called Mrs. Walton as Ann ran to look. There was a pink pig straddling another. She thought they were fighting. The rain dripped from the brim of her velour hat. "Come away," shouted Mrs. Walton, face white with excitement. The larger pig scrabbled on hind legs, its trotters, like high-heeled shoes, jigging up and down among the potato peelings and the mud. Mrs. Walton caught Ann by the belt of her mackintosh and tugged her back from the wall. She said pigs were absolutely animal in their behaviour. She said they were disgusting.

"You didn't even attempt to disguise what you were up to with Gerald," Mrs. Walton said.

"It's not unusual," Ann retorted, "to enjoy making love to one's fiancé. We're not living in the middle ages. Everyone does it now."

"Rubbish," cried Mrs. Walton. "Not everyone. There's such a thing as self-control."

At the thought of the self-control she had been forced to exercise the night before, Ann was filled with rage. "I do have self-control," she shouted. "I do. What do you think it was like for us with you calling out all the time?"

"You're nothing but a prostitute," said Mrs. Walton.

The fight went out of Ann. She was gazing at her mother's head bent over the suitcase, at the clean grey hairs beginning to show at the roots, at the dyed red curls quivering about her cheeks.

"I don't take money for it," she said forlornly, and she tried to touch her mother's arm to reassure her that she was loved, but Mrs. Walton sprang away from her with dilated eyes.

"Don't touch me," she cried out, running into the sitting room and snatching up her stockings, her handbag and the packet of humbugs she had bought for the train.

O Hell, thought Ann, I'll have to beg now, and

13

she looked at her mother standing there in the centre of the room, her bare feet planted on the carpet, her toe-nails painted raspberry red.

"Don't go Mummy, please don't go." She couldn't bear the guilt that would follow if Mrs. Walton left abruptly: the sniffing in the bedroom as she snapped the catches on the suitcase, the pathetic sighings as she dressed for the journey, the disgruntled face in the doorway as she departed for Brighton and the clean sea air. Ann felt very sad and tired suddenly. She sank to her knees on the floor and tears spilled from her eyes.

Neither of them heard Mrs. Kershaw come into the flat. She wore sandals summer and winter and she padded about the house like a cat. With her gypsy earrings and her peasant blouse, she bounced into the room. She stopped appalled.

"The door was open," she began. "Do excuse me."

She fled out on to the landing at once, leaving Ann still on her knees and her mother clutching her bedjacket to her breast.

"You foolish girl," said Mrs. Walton, recovering. "Whatever will Mrs. Kershaw think. Get up and behave yourself. I'm sick to death of your dramatics." And she went angrily into the bedroom.

"Mrs. Kershaw won't mind," said Ann, following her. She stood there dejectedly, her face sullen.

In the end Mrs. Walton said she must go back to Brighton. She couldn't possibly stay as there was a dance at the Wine Society and she needed to go to the hairdresser's. She touched the pale roots of her hair and struggled into her girdle. The carnations fell to the floor. Ann thought she was probably telling the truth. Her mother had never intended to stay; she was just getting her own back for not being taken to the party.

Ann made breakfast and they talked about Gerald's job in the States and about Mrs. Munro's daughter. Throughout, Mrs. Walton shifted on her chair as though aching from fatigue. "I'm so tired," she complained, and they both knew why but refrained from mentioning the farmyard noises that had kept her awake.

Ann took her in a taxi to the station and Mrs. Walton allowed herself to be kissed on the cheek.

"Give my love to father," said Ann.

There was the expected moment on the platform as the train began to crawl away with the little displeased face, lonely at the carriage window.

When she returned home Ann knocked at Mrs. Kershaw's door. Mrs. Kershaw was preparing food in the kitchen. Though she was a vegetarian, she wore a butcher's apron over her black skirt.

"Ah, Ann," she said. "I'm so glad you've come. I've a favour to ask." She wanted Ann to go up to the school tomorrow for a religious service. She herself worked irregular hours for a newspaper and wouldn't be able to go. "You have got two weeks' holiday," she observed, "and the children are terribly fond of you."

Ann couldn't refuse her. Mrs. Kershaw never said a word about people coming to stay—not like some landladies—and she must have known that sometimes Gerald had stayed all night. It was a nuisance though, having to put off all the jobs she'd intended doing: there were the sheets to collect from the laundry, the smears of soap and dried up toothpaste to be removed from the glass shelf in the bathroom, the cooker to clean—Ann had meant to take the whole thing apart and scrub round the gas jets. Not that Pamela was all that fussy—she spent most of her time away in Clapham—but she might mention at home that the flat looked untidy, and that was bound to get back to Mrs. Walton, who would then ring up and say Ann had made her feel ashamed. Mrs. Walton herself was shortsighted; she'd boiled coffee the night before and the milk had spilled over.

"It's a Harvest Festival Service," said Mrs. Kershaw. "You'll enjoy the singing."

It amazed Ann that Mrs. Kershaw, who held such strong views, should send her children to a Parochial school with a vicar coming in twice a week to take morning prayers. You'd have thought she might have preferred one of those progressive places where the teachers were called by their christian names and told to shut up. Perhaps it was a question of money. Ann didn't think Mrs. Kershaw was right in saying that the children liked her. "Tolerated" would have been a better word. Ann didn't care much for them either; she thought them tiresome and opinionated. Mrs. Walton said she could never understand how a well-spoken woman like Mrs. Kershaw had produced such dreadful offspring. "Their language," she said. "You'd think they were in the Merchant Navy."

Not to mention the second-hand clothing they wore.

"Do make certain," said Mrs. Kershaw, "that my jar of chutney is on display." She had made fourteen pounds of chutney several months before, but neither Roddy nor the children would touch it. "If it isn't, go and see if Jasper has left the bloody thing in the cloakroom."

Ann said she would. She hovered at the table and wondered whether to mention the scene with her mother. She stared at a small painting on the wall, in an elaborate frame, depicting a man and woman making love on a railway line. There was no sign of a train.

"My mother's gone," she said. "To Brighton. We had a row . . . about Gerald."

Mrs. Kershaw listened attentively; beneath the embroidered roses her heart beat with sympathy. She chopped some french beans and sprinkled them with salt. She said, "You mustn't be too hard on her, Ann dear. She's a very ordinary woman. How can she understand the way we all live? We inhabit a different world." And she gave a small satisfied smile.

Ann felt it was funny that anyone should call Mrs. Walton ordinary. It wasn't an adequate word. She thought of her mother's piano playing, her scheming, her ability to read French, the strength of her convictions, the inflexibility of her dreadful will. The way she advised Ann to wear make-up—"Exploit yourself more," she was given to saying; "paint your face." As if Ann were a Red Indian. The way she referred to men as "persons." Her use of the possessive pronoun. The subjectivity of her every thought. However, she said, "You're right, Mrs.

Kershaw." She went upstairs yawning and found the carnations lying under the bed. Perhaps she had been a little hard on her mother. She could have just apologised for keeping her awake and denied that Gerald had been in the flat. She could have said a stray dog had got into the house and run up and down the stairs barking. Her mother wouldn't have believed it, but the lie would have been appreciated.

*

Her first impression was that she had been mistaken for someone else. She looked behind her but there was no one in the open doorway. The stranger was beckoning and indicating the empty chair beside his own. His eyes held such an expression of certainty and recognition that she began to smile apologetically. It was as if he had been watching the door for a long time and Ann had kept him waiting. She did notice, as she excused herself along the row of seated mothers, that he had yellow curls and a flattish nose like a prizefighter. He was dressed appallingly in some sort of sweater with writing on the chest. On his feet he wore very soiled tennis shoes without laces.

He spoke when she sat down, though she couldn't catch what he said. Ann remembered seeing him before, one day last summer when she had fetched the children. She had noticed him at the time because she thought how foolish he looked—a large overgrown boy with rounded buttocks kicking a ball about the playground.

She could feel the blood rushing to her cheeks;

everyone was watching them, thinking she was a Mummy come straight from the office and he a Daddy devotedly snatching a moment away from the building site. Mrs. Kershaw's Jasper was grinning at her; he had an army cap pulled down over his eyes and he was unravelling the braid from a crumpled school blazer. All through the singing of "We Plough the Fields and Scatter" the stranger was fingering the material of her green suit jacket: the shoulder, the pocket flap, the edge of the lapel.

"That's a lovely bit of cloth," he hissed. And then a question—"Is it Donegal tweed?"

She didn't know; but it seemed hardly possible, looking the way he did, that he was an expert from the clothing industry, so she nodded and fixed her eyes on the row of children sitting cross-legged on the stage.

Though it was October, the sun shone through the high windows of the hall; the children tilted their heads to avoid the glare. Blurred and golden, they played idly with glittering strands of hair, located their parents, nudged each other and giggled silently. After the second verse the smaller children gave up singing altogether and watched the dust spiralling to the roof. They gazed dreamily upward, sucking their thumbs.

"That's flesh of my flesh," said the stranger, tugging at her elbow.

Try as she might she could not see which infant resembled him. Or rather, which did not. They were all beginning to look the same, flaxen-haired and snub-nosed, rocking now from side to side, eyes turned up to heaven. She felt slightly unwell. How

19

else to explain the particular degree of agitation and palpitation that she was experiencing? Perhaps she had the beginnings of a temperature. Even when they hunched over their knees for the prayers, he still plucked little pieces of fluff from her sleeve.

"Please," she whispered. "I'm praying."

"I'm all in favour of that," he said, sliding from the metal chair on to his knees. The yellow ringlets bounced, exposing a white neck and a small brown mole just visible above the ragged curve of his jumper.

One of those dramatic-looking Hampstead parents, enveloped in a black coat, was staring at Ann. She was winding a lock of hair round and round her finger. Ann didn't know whether to smile or not. It could have been somebody she'd met at Mrs. Kershaw's—all her friends looked very intelligent and did things in the theatre or made pottery—but she couldn't be sure. She started to tremble. There on the stage squatted the identical rows of children, flesh of his flesh, caught in a sunbeam. She had felt rather like this five years ago after an inoculation for polio before going to Spain with a girl from the office. At the time she'd expected to die. In the end she didn't go away because Mrs. Walton took her to Hastings, but she'd had splitting headaches and a temperature of 104, so it was probably a good thing she'd stayed in England.

The vicar was saying how nice it had been that they'd come along. His face was out of focus. She had to clench her hands in her lap to stop her fingers fluttering up and down. He thanked them for their offerings; he pointed proudly at the trestle table, the pyramid of tinned soup, the home-made cake, the polythene bag dewy with condensation, containing potatoes. A father, dressed as a life-boat-man in a P.V.C. jacket, stamped his waders on the wooden floor and shouted "Bravo." Ann couldn't identify Mrs. Kershaw's offering of chutney amongst so many others.

They had to stay exactly where they were until the children had filed back to their classrooms. Emily wouldn't look at her, but Jasper punched her on the shoulder as he passed. When they rose from their seats the stranger was close behind. She felt his hand on her shoulder, then her waist. She half turned her head, and his mouth brushed her hair. There was cinnamon on his breath.

Outside in the playground, he ran ahead. Hands in his pockets and shoulders hunched about his ears, he stood at the gate and barred the way.

"We'll have a cup of coffee," he said. "Down the road."

He wouldn't let her through. There was a confusion of women pushing prams, and a dog that ran in and out trailing a lead.

"There's things I have to do," she told him.

He was jogging up and down now on the tips of his toes—people were forced to squeeze past them. He had rosy cheeks and pale blue eyes that watched her face.

"Never," he said, and he took her arm and walked her away.

She couldn't eat the chocolate éclair he ordered. She was wondering how she could possibly be ill with Pamela coming to stay.

"I don't feel awfully well," she said. "It feels like the flu."

"Forget it," he advised. He was cramming cake between his slightly swollen lips, bending his head low over the plate. Even so there were crumbs all over the cloth.

"My fiancé," she told him, "is a great believer in honey and lemon."

It wasn't true—she had never known Gerald when ill—but she wanted him to know that she was engaged and wasn't the sort of girl who allowed herself to be picked up by strange men. He didn't seem to have heard; he was looking down at his plate thoughtfully. He wasn't handsome like Gerald; he was soft and rounded, and he irritated her because she wanted to go home and clean the cooker. She knew she was watching him in a calculating way; she could feel how hard her face had become. Her knees had stiffened. She was staring at him quite rudely, one eyebrow raised in the manner of Mrs. Walton when expressing contempt. She put her hand to her brow in case he glanced upwards. But he didn't. After a moment he said, "Do you remember the vegetables?"

"Vegetables?"

"The cauliflowers on the altar steps . . . those purple cabbages."

"Purple?"

"Do you not remember the loaves plaited to look like sheaves of corn?"

"Bread's not a vegetable," she said, though she had begun to remember the Harvest Festivals of her childhood—the choir in cassocks frilled at the neck, the lighted candles, D-Day dahlias in the pulpit, the smell of earth and wax, the whole church garlanded with fruit and flowers.

"Swedes," he said. "Parsnips, onions, marrow—"

"Carrots—"

"Ah," he said. "Those tender carrots with the leaves like young ferns."

Once she'd been to a Wordsworth evening at work, organised by the Poetry Society. Her friend Olive said she would enjoy it. When they wandered lonely as a cloud she wanted to scream with embarrassment. But *he* said things properly.

"Chrysanthemums," she told him. "Michaelmas daisies."

"Michaelmas daisies?" he repeated wonderingly.

"Don't you remember?"

"Michaelmas daisies," he said again. "You've got a lovely turn of phrase."

She'd stopped trembling. It wasn't like talking to somebody at work or to Mrs. Kershaw; she didn't have to keep nodding and watching mouths to know when it was her turn. She told him she'd been living in London for two years, that she worked for the BBC. She was slightly breathless and spoke as if she were running at the same time. People came in and out, chairs were moved, dishes gathered up on trays, but it was happening at a great distance; she concentrated entirely on his pink face crowned with foppish curls. It wasn't that he asked her questions —he hardly said a word for several minutes—rather that she felt compelled to talk. She didn't say anything particularly memorable, that was the funny part of it. Nothing to compare with the Michaelmas daisies. She said she didn't really know she was living in London, it could have been anywhere—she moved around on public transport to places that were names on maps, she travelled the underground system, she went up lifts at Bush House, she ate in sandwich bars; at the weekend she sometimes walked on the Heath with Olive.

He might have been a doctor listening to the symptoms of some obvious disease, sitting there with eyes half-closed, nodding, murmuring an assent, rubbing the side of his snub nose with the edge of his finger. She told him Mrs. Kershaw went out to work; she implied that she herself would never neglect her children for the sake of a career. She was going to take Jasper and Emily to the swimming baths at Swiss Cottage after school tomorrow. She didn't swim herself because she grew hysterical every time the water drew level with her heart. Wasn't that odd, considering she had been brought up beside the sea?

He ate her éclair, ordered more coffee. Now and then he wiped his lips on his torn sleeve. Once he repeated her name—"Ann"—as if he was biting on something, and when his mouth widened there were spaces between his teeth. She told him about her cousin coming to stay, how she had to fetch the clean sheets from the laundry. She started to describe Pamela's character, certain mannerisms that were irritating. "When she eats something . . . like a piece of cheese . . . that sort of thing . . . she holds it in both hands and nibbles on it. Of course, there's no reason why she shouldn't . . . we're all different . . . but all the same . . ."

He looked up then, unsmiling, and she saw re-flected in his eye the microscopic image of the tea urn on the counter. In the middle of a sentence she detected the note of malice in her voice. She actually began to stutter; she couldn't continue. She had never before experienced such a feeling of unworthiness. All the things she had told him, the boring trivia that had bubbled up from her mind, the stupid assertion that there was a right and a wrong way to eat a piece of cheese. Whatever was the matter with her? He wasn't watching her critically; he was looking down at the table again, sweeping his fingers back and forth across the cloth, pushing a small wall of crumbs. She had to put her hand over her mouth to stop the other words coming out, the vulgar resentments—Gerald leaving her, the flowers her mother hadn't wanted, Pamela and her visits to Clapham—all the confidential details of her life that suddenly sickened her. She wanted to be good.

They sat for a moment in silence. Then he told her his name—William McClusky. He was a playwright. Both statements for some reason caused her distress. His voice was light in pitch, thin and brutal-sounding on occasions, but she hadn't realised he was Scottish. He said he was "West Coast," whatever that might mean. Eventually, she supposed, with that accent it would mean her mother and father would find him common. Not officer class. She was puzzled that she should think her parents might meet him; she couldn't understand why she was upset at the idea of his being a writer of plays. What did it matter what he did? It was none of her business. And yet she was suffering. She stared at him in bewilderment.

"Are you?" she said.

Maybe he was lying to her. He didn't seem educated enough to be a writer. The few people she had met in the canteen of Bush House, who worked for Talks Programmes, had all come down from Oxford with degrees in Economics.

"I've a play in rehearsal at the moment. If it goes well when we take it to the provinces, there'll be a space at the Haymarket."

"How lovely."

She spoke flatly to disguise what she was feeling. She had only just met him and yet she didn't want him to go away into the provinces, away on trains, away from her. She was becoming confused. It must have something to do with Gerald leaving for America and her mother going back to Brighton—everyone going on journeys. Or she was ill.

"I'm on television tonight. Sort of an interview. Asking what it means to be a writer."

"My fiancé," she began, "is a lecturer in—"

"Will you watch me, then?" he asked.

"I haven't got a television set."

"I'll get you one. Tell me where you live and I'll have a friend of mine bring one round."

He wrote her address on the back of his hand. She was appalled that she had given it to him. She didn't want anyone bringing her a television, not with Pamela arriving and all the things she had to do before tomorrow. Not that she imagined he meant it.

He walked with her to the corner of the road. She

was shaking so much she kept knocking her ankles together and stumbling. He didn't seem to notice. He walked at the edge of the pavement, scuffing at the leaves with his tennis shoes.

"I'm away to the churchyard," he said. "To look at the graves."

She wondered if someone close to him had died recently. She didn't know what to say.

"That man of yours," he suddenly asked. "Is he out of work?"

"Out of work?"

"Could he not afford to buy a ring for your finger?"

They had come to the top of the hill and he began to dart round her in a circle, dribbling an imaginary ball.

"He had to go away to America," she protested. "There wasn't time." It hurt that it wasn't only her mother who thought Gerald hadn't come up to scratch.

"If you were my woman," he said. "You'd have a ring for your finger." And in broad daylight he took her left hand in both of his—her address tatooed in ink on his wrist—and kissed her at the edge of her mouth.

*

He did send a television set. Two young men carried it up the stairs and put it on the window ledge. They didn't pass on a message or anything, which meant she spent all evening trying to find the right programme, and she hardly had a moment to tidy the flat for Pamela. The picture kept sliding out of view and coming up at the bottom again, and she saw so many bits out of so many films that she was exhausted and her eyes ached. Just when she feared she had missed him altogether and she'd switched from some cowboys shooting each other to death, there was quite a clear image of two men seated at a table. One of them was William. He wore a collar and tie and his hair was brushed back from his forehead. The other man was asking a question about contemporary British drama and William said, "Are you referring to that *Look Back in Anger* stuff?" At least, Ann thought those were his words, and she was in a position to understand him more than most, because she could still hear his voice in her head from earlier that day. She couldn't think anyone else understood; his accent had broadened incredibly. At any rate, the interviewer never answered; he leant forward in his chair, and there was a pause, and then he thanked William for coming along. William gave an abrupt little nod, and there was a close-up of him sitting there with his lower lip thrust out aggressively, more like a boxer than a writer. Then he faded out to loud background music.

She switched off the set and the picture folded inward; for a second there was a little white hole in the centre and then there was nothing but greyness and the outline of the kitchen door reflected in the screen. She knelt on the carpet and rocked backwards and forwards. Now that he had gone she couldn't remember what he looked like. She could see Gerald in her mind: the way he screwed up one eye when he blew out smoke, the slightly hooked nose, the two fingers he placed flat against his puckered mouth when he was thinking about something. She could see her mother, all of her, at one of her bridge evenings, holding the cards to her breast like a fan, and the watch-strap too tight on her plump arm. She even remembered the crumpled face of the woman at the laundry when she collected the sheets. But she couldn't see William at all.

She must have knelt in front of the television for ages, because when she heard Mrs. Kershaw calling, her knees hurt as she got up from the floor. She was so stiff she nearly fell over.

Mrs. Kershaw was standing half way up the stairs, wearing a flowered dressing-gown tied round the waist with string.

"Telephone," she said.

Ann dreaded lest it was her mother; she was not in the mood to be reproached. Her mother would say "Hello stranger," regardless of the fact that Ann had seen her two days previously. "Daddy thought I looked very peaky when I came home from you." And Ann would say "Hello Mummy." Then Mrs. Walton would ask with dreadful perception, "What's wrong with you? What's going on?"

She picked up the phone and said carefully, "Hello."

"Did you watch, then?"

"Oh I did . . . I did."

"I'm glad. I wanted you to."

"Oh I did . . . I did."

The wall was painted dark green like a public convenience. There was a card with the number of a taxi service and a typed notice saying that foreign coins should not be used. She could hear her breath echoing round and round the mouthpiece of the telephone.

"Well then," he said. "That's all right." And he rang off.

*

Her cousin Pamela arrived the next day in time for lunch. She stood inside the porch with her lips slightly parted, as if she was bothered about something and was thinking of the right question. She had thin, perfectly straight eyebrows that almost met in the middle, and delicately tinted cheeks. And never thought of her as being pretty until she saw her, and always it took her by surprise.

"My God," said Pamela as soon as Ann opened the door. "You look worn out. Whatever have you been up to?"

She carried a suitcase and two carrier bags and she said the stairs would kill her. She made an awful racket in the hall and Ann was worried about Mrs. Kershaw's friend, Roddy, coming out and complaining. He had once, a year ago, when Olive tripped over the mat, and he'd appeared, practically naked, waving his arms about. Olive had nearly died laughing. When Ann apologised later to Mrs. Kershaw, she said Roddy had a damn nerve and not to take any notice. Still, she didn't want to draw attention to herself, or to Pamela for that matter.

Pamela only came to visit when she wanted somewhere cheap to stay. Usually she went out every night and on occasions hadn't returned till the afternoon. She told the most hair-raising stories about the friends she had in Clapham. Ann never understood why she couldn't stay with them, seeing they were so friendly. They had a living room painted completely black, and they slept on cushions on the floor, so it wasn't a question of there not being enough beds. Ann had never really liked her, which was strange as she was rather like Mrs. Walton in a way—vivacious and full of fun when she was in a good mood. She made Ann feel clumsy. All the photographs in the family album showed them together at the seaside with bucket and spade— Pamela, small and dark, smiling into the camera, and Ann, tall and fair, staring down at the sand with her bony toes curled inwards. Pamela was always hinting that things were not as they seemed. When she was fifteen she had said that Ann's father had put his arm round her in the greenhouse. Ann thought she was disgusting and told her so. Pamela had laughed and said, "What's disgusting about it? It's normal." If she hadn't meant there was something odd about Captain Walton's gesture of affection among the geraniums, why bother to mention it at all? Ann wasn't close to her father. He had been in the regular army—her mother had married him on the rebound from an airman she met on the Isle of Wight—and he was twenty years older than she. He'd enjoyed the war and Mrs. Walton said he wasn't the same man once it was won. They'd lived in married quarters up and down the country—a succession of brick bungalows with concrete garages stained by the rain, and newly planted bushes withering beside concrete paths. They sent Ann away to school; and when that was over and Captain Walton had retired, Ann scarcely knew him. He was now erect and frail. He often didn't answer when spoken to. Mrs. Walton was fond of saying his mind had gone on manoeuvres. Ann wondered what she might have been like had her father been that rear-gunner—reckless, in her mother's memory—and not the elderly man walking the pier at Brighton. Old soldiers, she knew, never died; in her father's case she felt it was not so much that he was fading away, as that he had never been there in the first place. She did watch him at Christmas, after being told of the incident in the greenhouse, but he didn't seem to notice Pamela. He sat straight-backed in his armchair by the electric fire and read his book on Rommel.

"Oh," said Pamela, as soon as she entered the sitting room. "I see you've got a television set."

"It's on loan," said Ann. She started to prepare the lunch, peeling the cooked beetroot and putting hot water and vinegar into a bowl. There wasn't any sugar. She'd taken a list out shopping, but when she went into the supermarket she hadn't been able to concentrate on what she was doing; she'd forgotten all sorts of things.

Pamela told her she was thinking of applying for a job in London—it was time she broke new ground: her friend in Clapham thought she was a fool to bury herself at the seaside. She wanted to find something more suited to her talents . . . she fancied herself as an amateur psychologist . . . maybe she could get an opening in criminal records.

Ann looked down at her hands, stained crimson from the beetroot; she began to feel ill again. She'd been perfectly normal when she woke in the morning; the peculiar emotions of the night before had abated; she had eaten breakfast and passed to and fro in front of the television, and it was simply an object. She had even put the phone call from her mind. But now, with Pamela prattling on about finding herself, she could see the television protruding from the window ledge, its aerial pointing at the ceiling. It seemed to fill the room, blotting out her books, the glass of dying carnations, the photograph of her mother and father in its silver frame. Behind the curved eyeball of the screen was William. She had only to turn the switch and he'd be sitting there in a collar and tie, talking about drama. She wanted him back. She wanted to know what he looked like. She had to mention him.

"A man gave it to me," she said.

"Gave you what?" said Pamela. She was turning over a lettuce leaf as if to make sure Ann had washed it properly.

"He's a playwright . . . he was on a programme last night."

"On the television?"

"Yes."

She was watching Ann's face intently; she was very astute. "What sort of a man?"

"I've told you. A writer. He was waiting for me when I went into the church hall. He took me for coffee and we talked about his work and then—"

"Church hall! You were picked up in a church hall?"

Ann reddened. "Not picked up. He knew me."

"Oh."

Pamela impaled a slice of cold ham on the prong of her fork. She looked at it distastefully and rolled it into a heap under the lettuce leaf. She was like that; no matter what Ann did for her she never seemed to appreciate it.

"I thought," said Pamela, "you were engaged to an American."

Ann had forgotten about Gerald. Not once throughout a disturbed night had there been images of him.

"Gerald isn't American," she said.

Pamela knew perfectly well he was English, because Mrs. Walton, at the first opportunity, had told Auntie Bea everything about him. In the telling, Gerald had been promoted from lecturer to professor, but her mother hadn't altered his nationality.

"Where does this man live?" asked Pamela. "This playwright." As if she didn't believe he existed.

Ann said she didn't know.

"And he gave you a television set? Do you know how much they cost?"

She had a way of looking at Ann, assessing the price of the clothes she wore—she had always done so, even as a child—the kind of shoes she bought. Her scrutiny, Ann felt, like Mrs. Walton's, was tinged with hostility. She thought Ann too tall, too ungainly—that her hair needed shaping. She herself was five foot one. She went to a dressmaker in Lewes and had her clothes copied from up-to-the-minute magazines. She was wearing a dress like a gym-slip, and she had black knee-socks over her stockings. It was disconcerting for both of them, being related by blood. It was all right when Ann was with people at work, with Mrs. Kershaw, Olive. She could be herself, her away-from-home self. She could talk about sleeping with men and being left-wing. But with Pamela she was constrained. They had both been brought up within the same area of experience. Both had fled from their environment. They each listened with sharpened hearing to the note of affectation in the other's voice. Ann could go home to Brighton for the weekend and look at the women with their out-of-date dresses and bee-hive hair styles, and feel superior. She could listen to the sound of lawn mowers on a Sunday morning, seated on a deck chair in the garden; to the buzz of wasps, the clatter of car hoods, a radio somewhere over the trellis fence. She was there, but she was only visiting. She could bear it for the moment—the torment of being related to her mother and father, the wounding. She was waiting to go back to London, where she had no enemies—waiting for the retreat to be sounded. And it was the same for Pamela, even though she had not yet left home; it wasn't anything to do with geography. So it was no use putting on a show. They could never be friends.

"I didn't say he'd given it to me," Ann protested. "It's loaned."

"It's a very odd thing to do." Pamela was stabbing at the mess on her plate. "He must have got a funny impression of you. What was he doing in a church hall?"

"It was a school service. Mrs. Kershaw was at work and I went in her place. Somebody had to go. Her Roddy always stays in bed."

"But what about *him?* That man. What was he there for?"

"He was there for his children, of course."

The moment Ann said it, she realised he must be married. It hadn't occurred to her before. She'd forgotten about the flesh of his flesh and all that went with it. She looked down at her plate, and the pattern of flowers was blurred. She was crying.

"Oh crumbs," said Pamela, and she jumped up and pulled Ann's head to her gym-slip and stroked her hair. She was terribly kind and gentle. She stood crooning to her, "Don't cry . . . there . . . there."

"I'm sorry, Pamela," Ann said. "Ever since yesterday I've felt so ill. I must be due for the curse. Or I've got the flu." And she sniffed to prove it.

Pamela wiped her face with the tea-towel and made her a cup of coffee. There was no sugar, so neither of them could drink it.

Ann told her about William watching the door when she went into the school. She described his curls, the pinkness of his cheeks, the paleness of his eyes.

"Oh," said Pamela, "he sounds sweet." And she gave a wistful smile as if they were talking about a baby.

"He's got spaces between his teeth . . . you know . . . gaps."

"Spaces?" said Pamela. "Do you mean he's got teeth missing?"

They both began to laugh then. Ann cried at the same time.

"I don't really like men with curly hair," she confessed. "Do you?"

"Only if they've got all their teeth," said Pamela. And they lolled on their chairs at the kitchen table and snorted with laughter.

Ann felt weakened and relaxed; her voice became deeper and full of meaning. She told Pamela about William dancing round her at the top of the hill, the cars going downwards, the plane trees growing smaller in perspective as they reached the Finchley Road. "Almost bare of leaves," she said, "and when the cars drove by, people looked at us, and he began to circle round and round me . . . you know . . . tripping . . . like a prizefighter. Like somebody on the cinema."

"How do you mean?" Pamela said.

"Just before I went down the hill, he kissed me. On the side of my mouth."

"Where?"

"Then he rang me up and said he was glad I'd watched him."

"How do you mean?" Pamela said again, but Ann was talking about Gerald now, reliving the farewell party and pushing him out of the flat.

"He wanted me to take *all* my clothes off, but how could I? The smell of his breath too . . . it was awful."

"There's something I ought to tell you," said Pamela. "I've come down for a reason."

"I didn't like the way he was so rough with me. I

mean, we've been to bed several times, but I don't know how I feel. He should have taken me with him to America."

"I'm late with my period," said Pamela. "Two months."

But Ann didn't hear her. She was thinking of Mrs. Walton shouting from the bedroom.

"How would you feel," she asked, "if your mother started calling out?"

Pamela was drumming the tips of her fingers on the table and staring out of the window. She seemed to have lost interest.

"She came down to meet Gerald," continued Ann. "She kept calling out for water. When we went to the airport the next day, there wasn't time to say goodbye properly. I just tried to make him feel guilty. In the future I'll only have letters to go on. They're so impersonal. I'm supposed to fly out to him in February, but how can I? I don't really know him."

She didn't like Pamela knowing her engagement wasn't all moonlight and roses, but she had to tell someone. Pamela was looking at her now with contempt.

"The old bastard," she said.

"He's not old," said Ann. "He's only twenty six."

"Your mother," Pamela said. "Fancy landing on you the week he was leaving."

Ann was shocked that Pamela could be so brutal. She regretted instantly that she'd told her so much. Pamela had obviously missed the point and maybe she would repeat the entire conversation to her mother, who would then telephone Mrs. Walton.

"You won't tell Auntie Bea anything, will you?" she begged. She hadn't meant to whine but she dreaded lest her mother hear about the television set.

Pamela didn't reply. She sat there scraping her thumb nail on the tablecloth.

"Please," Ann pleaded. All at once her mouth started to tremble—she bit her lip and her cheeks wobbled—she was actually crying again.

This time Pamela wasn't sympathetic. She said coldly, "You know what's wrong with you, don't you? It's nothing to do with the flu or getting a period." She thumped her fist on the table as if it was obvious, and the cold coffee leapt in the cups.

Ann stared at her with moist eyes. "What's wrong with me?" she asked.

"You've fallen in love with that toothless wonder you met at the church hall," said Pamela. "That's what's the matter with you." And she glared at Ann with her eyebrows set in one straight line.

She didn't help Ann to wash up; she went and sat in the sitting room and watched the television. First there was a story for the under-fives, then a programme in Welsh.

When Mrs. Kershaw's children came home from school, Pamela said she would come to the swimming baths. Usually she spent ages in the bathroom before dashing off to Clapham. She thought the children were very original; she admired their cast-off clothing and gave each of them a two shilling piece. The little girl was all over her. Ann had noticed before that Emily had a tendency to play-act; Mrs. Kershaw's Roddy was supposed to be an actor, and he often took the children to the theatre. Emily stroked Pamela's coat and fiddled with her necklace. She said she was pretty. She borrowed a bathing costume of her mother's for Pamela and they went into the changing room together. Ann sat upstairs in the onlookers' gallery.

The swimming coach was covered in a rash; he was so busy scratching he'd never have noticed anyone going down for the third time. He padded up and down with his feet turned out and his chest inflamed. It was probably something to do with the chlorine, Ann thought: everyone spent a penny in the water and they overdid the chemical to kill the germs. There was a pregnant lady teaching her two-year-old to be afraid of nothing. She had long red hair that turned black in the water and trailed out behind her like seaweed; the child kept screaming and scrabbling upwards in her arms to be out of the wet. Ann wondered if they put dye in the pool, until she saw it was a reflection of the tiled floor: it was blue like the sky in a picture postcard. The roof was set with great panes of glass—everything shimmered with light: the tiled walls, the surface of the pool, the white arches leading to the changing cubicles.

Pamela looked nice in Mrs. Kershaw's costume. She had a very pale skin and heavy sloping shoulders and she'd left on her necklace, the one from Turkey, hung with little silver coins. She sat down on the edge of the bath, Emily and Jasper dragging at her elbows, and searched for Ann in the gallery. She waved. She nudged the children and pointed, but they didn't look in the right direction. While they were squinting upwards, a boy ran out of a cubicle and jumped clean over them, with knees raised, and landed in the pool. The water bounced straight up into the air and curved over. Pamela shifted on her haunches and wiped her face with her hands. She stretched one foot out and flopped clumsily downwards. The children dog-paddled in a circle. After a few moments Pamela struck out towards the deep end, head turning from side to side, as if she couldn't get comfortable, shoulders rolling, her pale arms lifting. When she reached the rail she heaved herself on to the tiles and lay on her belly, stranded, water streaming away from her white legs. She sat upright and blew her nose in her fingers.

It was then Ann saw William. He was standing with his hands on his hips, looking up at her. He wore a pair of black swimming trunks and his hair was flat to his head. For one moment Ann stopped breathing and the next she wanted to hide. She thought everyone else was free and undressed, while she was cumbersome and conspicuous in her grey coat and her court shoes. She was even holding a bag; it was dangling over the rail, bulky with her documents and Emily's headband. She almost let go of it. She had never really liked nudity—all that expanse of flesh touched by the grave—unless you'd been away on holiday and become less obscene. But he looked beautiful, outlined in light that seemed to waver and coalesce, though she knew it was only the reflection of the glass roof on the water. There was so much noise and movement: the screaming, the splashing, the mouths opening in one great shout, the putty-coloured bodies plunging from the diving board. A wave of sound and light rose up and engulfed her. She felt she was drowning.

He took them to have tea in a café on the Finchley Road. Ann didn't remember how they got there; it was quite a long walk and there was a lot of traffic. The children chattered and Pamela carried the wet towels. When they sat down at the table he just stared at Ann. She didn't mind him staring, as she would have done had it been Gerald or some stranger. She was so happy she couldn't stop smiling. His eyes were bloodshot and his hair was drying and beginning to curl again. Pamela had found a piece of wool in her pocket and she played cat's cradle with the children.

"Pamela's come to stay," Ann told him.

"Aye, I know," he said. He knew she wanted him to include Pamela just for a moment. "I hope you have a pleasant stay."

"Thank you," said Pamela in a subdued voice. Ann wondered where all her social ease had gone. Her face was blotchy and her fashionable clothes looked rather silly. Her gloves, lying on the table, had a row of holes across the knuckles.

After Ann had drunk her tea he reached forward and dropped something into her cup.

"For you," he said. "From my pinkie."

She didn't know what he meant. There was a silver ring, perfectly plain, at the bottom of the cup.

"Whatever is it?" she asked, and she lifted it up, sticky at the edge with sugar.

He took it from her and held up her left hand and slid the ring down her finger.

Pamela was crouched over the web of wool with her hair crumpled on her collar. She was looking at Ann with her mouth open, and her eyes were bloodshot too, stained with pink, and watering. And for the first time in all their lives she was watching Ann timidly.

"Isn't that beautiful," Ann said, twisting her hand about to show the silver ring. Under the table he was stroking her knee and smiling—smiling, just as she was.

She didn't remember leaving the café. She knew he hailed a taxi and they sat on the two tip-down seats. Pamela was there, wedged opposite with her hands still trapped in the cat's cradle of wool, and the children, one on either side of her, limp on the leather seating, with towels in their arms and pale knees bunched together. It was dark in the sky and there were pockets of light in the busy streets. Shadows ran across William's face. The taxi stopped and jolted and crawled forward amidst the line of cars going out of the city to Golders Green. Shut outside in the October night the people swarmed over the crossings and ran dementedly for buses; they leapt towards the moving platforms and swung like rag dolls from the glittering rails. It felt like Christmas —the lighted windows, the extravagant journey, the silver ring encircling her finger. William didn't come into the house; she didn't invite him because she knew if he wanted to he would have said.

"I'll see you very soon," he told her.

The children ran over the gravel. Beyond the privet hedge she could hear the taxi with him inside change gear as it climbed the hill.

"Hang your coat up," she said to Pamela, when they were in the flat. Pamela had flung it on to the sofa with the wet towels and her gloves.

There wasn't an atom of tenderness in Ann at this first moment of love. Now that he had gone she wasn't happy or grateful or bewildered. If anything, she felt anger. Until now it was as if she had been wrapped in strips of cloth like an Egyptian mummy. Every year, time had unwound another layer. At the very end of her life she would have lain exposed in the air and fallen away to dust. But William had cut through the bandages with one stroke, and she'd tumbled out perfectly preserved and ready to live. And he should have been with her. She didn't care if he was married or wore scruffy clothes. Pamela was right; she loved him.

Pamela was staring at her too. She was unwinding a thread of blue wool from her thumb.

"What's the matter?" Ann asked. "Cat got your tongue?"

She couldn't help being nasty. She went to the window and looked down into the shadowy garden. Last month Mrs. Kershaw had cut off the heads of the roses; she'd taken down the badminton net, and nobody went onto the grass. There was a model living on the ground floor in the flat behind Mrs. Kershaw. In the summer she had come out among the rose bushes to be photographed by the press— drawing in her breath and striking poses, head back, chin tilted upward to the branches of the sycamore tree. Ann had been jealous of her—of the abundance of her black hair and of the attention she received. But she wasn't jealous now. She had William.

The lights were on in the houses down Frognal, square after square: six flats to a house, each with a kitchen and a table laid for two.

How long was very soon?

"Who is he?" asked Pamela. She sounded terribly tired.

"I've told you. He's a writer."

"How many times have you met him?"

Ann didn't answer. She was wondering what a pinkie was. "What did he mean," she said. "when he called it a pinkie?" She held up her hand.

"It's slang," Pamela said. "It means a little finger. Queers put rings on them."

It's not true, thought Ann. How would she know something like that?

"I'm worried," said Pamela. "It's not like you. Your mother would have a fit."

But Ann didn't care. All that had happened to her before, in the past, when she had been like herself, had been a mistake. The assistant bank manager, the married man at the BBC, the painter she met on the Heath, even Gerald. Her mother had had a fit about all of them, with the exception of Douglas, the married man, who she hadn't known existed. It wasn't any use choosing someone for her mother to like; that was impossible. This time no one was going to interfere or spoil anything, or make her behave in any way that wasn't real.

Pamela didn't go to Clapham. She made a telephone call and came back upstairs with her mascara smeared, as if she had been weeping. She ran the bath and was in there for over an hour. She kept lifting the plug out and refilling the bath, and there was a clinking noise at one point, as though she had knocked something from the glass shelf.

"Have you broken anything?" shouted Ann, but Pamela didn't reply. Selfishly she turned the tap full on and ran the hot-water cylinder cold.

Ann sat in the kitchen and looked at the silver ring. She thought about all the things people said to each other, the words they were in the habit of repeating and the words they always left out. He hadn't talked to her at great length . . . he'd only stared at her. He had said, "If you were my woman." Now that she had his ring, did it mean that she was? Why hadn't he said something important, memorable, when he dropped it into her cup? She fretted at the table, unsure now that he was out of her sight. She thought about babies in prams, the mowing of lawns, the preserving of houses. What opportunities everyone had to be happy: the time spent together, the golf clubs in the hall, the man's razor in the cupboard. She couldn't see William in a peaked cap walking across the green at home, but anything was possible now. Would he want to marry her? Would there be a wedding, after he got divorced, and would her father wear his dress uniform and his medals? Her parents didn't know anybody who had even separated, let alone divorced, so it wasn't going to be easy. Her mother would be furious at being outdone by Mrs. Munro: the west coast of Scotland could hardly be compared with California.

Mrs. Kershaw came up to thank her for looking after the children.

"Pamela did that," Ann said.

"They mentioned Pamela," said Mrs. Kershaw. She sat down heavily on a chair, and Pamela came out from the bathroom in her dressing gown, the ends of her hair all wet and her face perspiring. She was so tired she could hardly walk straight. She flopped onto the sofa, her eyes glittering.

"I wouldn't have thought," said Ann, "you needed a bath after all that swimming."

Pamela shrugged. For a moment she resembled Mrs. Walton. She looked put out, offended by something. A memory came into Ann's head of a station platform at Lewes. Her mother and father had been to a luncheon—something to do with Captain Walton's regiment—and she had been staying with Pamela. Her father was unusually talkative and his face was mottled. He complained of the heat and took off his army jacket. Mrs. Walton told him to pull himself together and she boarded the train and sat down in the compartment. When the whistle blew Father was still attending to his coat, staggering round and round trying to catch the end of his broad brown belt. The train drew out leaving him on the platform. Ann started to say something—she had the absurd notion they might never see him again—but her mother was sitting with her lips pressed together, staring at the flying trees and the fields. Then she shrugged, and the fur collar of her coat quivered about her indignant mouth. It was as if it had been she who had been left behind.

"Ann dear," said Mrs. Kershaw, and stopped.

Roddy was calling from downstairs. He was shouting that Ann was wanted on the telephone.

"You're wanted on the telephone," repeated Pamela, because Ann didn't move.

Roddy shouted louder. Even as Ann walked to the door, Mrs. Kershaw was rising from her chair to sit beside Pamela on the sofa. They had never met before.

Ann picked up the telephone receiver. "Hullo," she said.

"I've got things to attend to," said William.

"Aye, I know."

"I've got to go away."

"I see."

"Is there something wrong?" he asked. "Is there something bothering you?"

"I'm not bothered about anything," Ann said.

"Aye," he said. "You are."

"Your wife," she said. "The flesh of your flesh."

"Did I not tell you," he said. "I'm divorced from her."

Mrs. Kershaw's Roddy came out into the hall and made gestures at the ceiling. She stared at him. He jerked his thumb towards the stairs and mouthed at her. After a moment he went back into the flat and slammed the door.

"Are you still there?" asked William.

"Yes."

"When I see you, it'll be for good. You know what I mean?"

"I do," she said.

Going upstairs she thought of Gerald: how unlike William he was. Even on the telephone. Gerald could never be like William, not in a thousand years. He wouldn't have understood the question, let alone been able to give an answer. He was so cautious about everything. He hadn't the money for a ticket for her to go to America, and he wouldn't allow her to pay for herself. He couldn't marry her because he couldn't afford it, and he didn't want her to go out to work. He would send for her when it suited him. When next she saw William it would be forever.

Mrs. Kershaw and Pamela had been discussing her, Ann could tell. They watched her as she came through the door.

"Was it him?" asked Pamela.

Ann nodded.

"I've got the most dreadful feeling," Pamela said, hugging her knees on the sofa. She didn't say what the feeling was.

"I know what you think," said Ann. She was grinning so much the words sounded strangled. "I admit it's odd."

"He's . . . he's . . . ?" Pamela was having difficulty articulating.

"Yes," said Ann. "He's beautiful."

"Oh, he is," Pamela agreed. She sounded surprised. She looked at Mrs. Kershaw. "He really is."

"Does he go into the Nag's Head?" said Mrs. Kershaw.

"Does he?" prompted Pamela.

Ann looked at them.

"There's a man," said Mrs. Kershaw. "A poet. He's well known in Hampstead. He goes into pubs and he talks to women."

"It's possible," Ann said carefully, "that he writes poems."

"Are you sure?" asked Mrs. Kershaw, "that you know the sort of man he is?"

"Aye," said Ann. "He's my man." It sounded a little melodramatic, and she hoped Pamela wouldn't remember the musical that they had both seen in Brighton. There had been a heroine who, on hearing her lover singing in the distances—something about the morning mist being on the heather —had cried aloud "My Man" and bounded like a deer into the wings.

Self-consciously she went into the bathroom to wash, leaving Mrs. Kershaw and Pamela together, and found beside the lavatory bowl a cup and half-bottle of gin, practically empty.

2

William returned two days later, when Ann was sleeping. Pamela came into her bedroom and shook her by the shoulder.

"It's him," she said. "He's in the sitting room." She fled into the bathroom and locked the door.

Ann couldn't find her dressing gown. While she was wrapping the coverlet about her, she heard the music. He had put a record on the turntable and was standing by the window in his tennis shoes, wearing a discoloured raincoat.

"Oh, it's you," she said, and he put a finger to his lips and made a sshhing sound. She stood there, nervously pushing her hair back from her face and wishing she had a comb.

It was an endlessly long record that began with the plucking of strings. It reminded her of a cartoon film she had seen about a rabbit with buck teeth jumping along a field. She could hear a violin, sad and whining, and a piano in the background; there

51

was no tune to it at all. Every now and then it would reach some kind of climax. She would clear her throat in readiness to speak—and it would begin all over again, *tum te tum tum tum tum te,* loud in the sitting room, as if they were there in actuality, the men in black ties holding their instruments. It would never do to interrupt. Her own heart beat to the mournful throb of the violin.

William looked different: his hair was straighter, the colour had faded. He tapped his plimsoll on the carpet, and when he bent his head it was ash-grey and clipped all over. She had thought, after their last meeting, that when next she saw him he would take her in his arms, kneel at her feet. But he stayed detached, watching the black disc circling round and round. When the music finally ended, she was trembling all over. She was going to say how lovely it had been. She took a step towards him. He was turning the record on to the other side.

"You'll like this," he said.

Down went the stylus. Tenderly he let go of the arm and off went the plucking again, the leaping rabbit, the violins and the copycat piano. She was struggling not to laugh; she kept thinking of Pamela imprisoned in the bathroom. She studied the leg of a chair, conscious that he was watching her. This time, some instrument, deeper in tone than the rest, repeated a series of notes that the violin had played earlier. She began to catch the melody, jerking her head in time to the music.

"No, no," he said harshly. "Listen."

It wasn't fair—he had tapped his foot on the carpet: even now he was moving his hand in the air like

52

a maestro. She was sorry he had stopped her; she lost concentration almost immediately. All she could hear now was a melancholy voice singing "O dearie, O dearie," over and over. She shook with suppressed laughter and covered her face with her hands. When the music came to a conclusion, years later, he took hold of her wrists in the silent room and pulled her fingers away from her eyes. Her teeth were chattering.

"Now," he said. "Where do you lie down?"

She pointed in the direction of the bedroom and he went ahead of her. She followed with one hand held curiously behind her, fluttering like a shirt tail, as if she was signalling to someone for help.

"Pamela's in the bathroom," she told him.

"It's as good a place as any," he said, and she sat down on the side of the double bed still shrouded in the coverlet. He was taking off his raincoat, pulling his sweater up over his head. He was broad-shouldered, with a short full neck and small pale ears.

"Aren't you stopping?" he asked, and smiled.

She shuffled beneath the sheets and pushed the coverlet away from her, looking at his chest and the nipples like two brown raisins embedded in his pale skin. There were no preliminaries. Nor did he take any precautions. He didn't have a clean handkerchief ready under the pillow; there was no chemical apparatus such as she had often used with Gerald. He kissed her on the mouth and rolled on top of her. It was unreal for a time, before any words were said: the smell of him, the texture of his back, the roughness of his arms above the elbow, not knowing where to put her knees. It was such an intimate situation to be in and yet so infantile—nuzzling against the unfamiliar body, sucking mouths and squirming. She kept catching his ankle bone with her toe nail. Must cut them, she thought.

"I'm so sorry . . . I'm sorry."

He stuck his fingers in her ears and there was a roaring sound. She shook him away.

"Don't," she cried, as if he had perpetrated an outrage.

"I love you," he said.

"I love you," she repeated, and tears squeezed out of her eyes.

Afterwards he cradled her in his arms and patted her back like a child that needed comforting.

"That's good, isn't it?" he said. "It's what your mammy did to you when you were a babby."

"I suppose so," she agreed, though it almost hurt.

"What did you think," he asked, "when I first met you?"

"I thought I had the flu," she said.

She was trying to imagine her mother looking after her when she was little. She'd seen a photograph of herself in a fluffy bonnet and white leggings—her cheek pressed to her mother's, a toothless placating smile, one fat fist doubled at her neck.

"Why do mothers do it," she wanted to know, "the patting on the back?"

"It's continuity," he said. "We were grown under the heart."

The bedroom was painted pink: the window sills,

the walls. Mrs. Walton had donated a small pink rug to match. She had made it herself during the war—woven a ship on it with pink woolly sails and clouds floating. There was a basket chair with a satin cushion set beside the wardrobe. It was like a nursery, she thought, lying in his arms in the warm bed, with the ceiling washed blue, the plaster flaking above the light bulb. She wanted to tell him that she didn't jump into bed with everyone, but she couldn't think how to say it. It would sound as if she was apologising, as if she feared that already he despised her. But what did men think in their heads, the very first time, when it was over? She looked with creased face at the pink wall and heard Pamela unlock the door of the bathroom. William's arm lay beside hers on the top blanket. His was round and muscular, hers bony at elbow and wrist. Did he find her too thin and gawky? Or did he need that—seeing he was so sturdy and compact? Would it not be better if she were dimpled and curved like a woman in a painting? Her sense of inadequacy made her resentful. She stayed quite still, but inside she drew away. She frowned above the line of his bunched shoulder and stared at the wall steadfastly. Right from that first moment in the school hall, when he had beckoned her to the vacant seat beside his own, she had disliked him. She thought she still did, underneath it all; he was so sure of himself. She had been happier when he had indicated love, not practised it. He was stroking her tangled hair. He was thinking his private thoughts that didn't include her. His mind had gone on manoeuvres—why couldn't it be like the time in the swimming baths or in the café?

"Did you know we'd do this?" she asked. "I mean, so quickly."

"I don't know anything," he said.

His words filled her with panic. He was refusing to be committed. He was taking everything back— himself, the certainty in the taxi, the ring in her cup.

"I'm wearing it," she said, stretching her hand out to remind him. "Pamela says that queers wear them on their little fingers."

"She's off her head," he said scornfully. "I got it from Gus."

"I think it's beautiful."

"I've had it for five years," he said.

"Who's Gus?" She heard the critical inflection in her voice, similar to her mother's when she imagined she'd been slighted.

"A mate of mine. I came down from Scotland with him. We bought each other rings. I wanted you to have mine."

"Thank you," she said. But she didn't want the ring anymore. She didn't want anything belonging to this Gus. What were two grown men doing handing each other silver rings for their fingers?

"It's not only the public schools," he said, "who specialise in friendship between men. Do you like cowboy films?"

"Oh, yes," she said, though she didn't. It was always the same horse going round the same bend with the same stretch of desert ahead.

"That's where friendship began. Mates," William said. "In the West, when they didn't have any women."

She didn't think he meant it the way it sounded. He was being poetic, she felt, like when he said "Michaelmas daisies," over and over.

"You'll meet Gus. He's a likeable man. He lives with his girlfriend in Kentish Town."

"I'd love to meet him," she said politely, though it was the last thing she wanted and she didn't intend to feel affection for him.

"We used to sit in the wardrobe at home, when I was married. Sheila didn't like that. We used to squat among her dresses and sing folk songs. He's got a great voice."

He was filling her head with so many images, she couldn't sort them out: the name of his past wife, his house, the clothes on the hangers, him and Gus inside a cupboard singing together. It was an odd place to sit, surely.

She was restless and uncomfortable. There was the odour of sweat and something pungent and clinging, like fish glue. Even so, she was upset when he jumped out of bed and said he wanted a cup of tea. She had thought they might lie there for hours, dozing and chatting—and doing it again. He didn't mind at all about Pamela; he sauntered out into the sitting room, wearing only his trousers, and she heard them talking together.

Ann dressed with special care, though casually, so he wouldn't guess she was doing it for him. She wore her blue smock and she put blue eye-shadow on her lids. She rubbed it off again in case Pamela said, "What are you tarted up for?" She was surprised that her face hadn't altered—been plumped out with love and self-satisfaction. I love you, William, she told the bathroom glass. I really love you.

When she went into the sitting room he was on the sofa with his arm round Pamela. She was leaning her head against his shoulder.

"She's sick," he said. "She ought to have a hot bottle for her stomach."

"What's wrong with you?" asked Ann. She sat unwillingly beside Pamela and felt her forehead.

"She's pregnant," said William. "She did tell you."

Ann was going to deny it, but she half remembered Pamela talking about being late for a period.

"Oh dear," she said. "How awful. You poor thing."

She thought Pamela had confided in William rather too quickly. She couldn't imagine her telling Gerald anything so personal. She looked at William's arm about Pamela's shoulder and wanted to tear it away. God damn it, she thought, please leave her alone—stop holding her like that. She had to look down at the brocade material of the sofa, the fold in Pamela's dressing-gown, the one waxen shin shining bare above the bedroom slipper. She had to hide her eyes, the jealousy in them, the hatred of William. It wasn't her fault she was afraid of him: it was her mother's—her upbringing. She had been taught that men were different; she had digested the fact of their inferiority along with her banana sandwiches and her milk. Men were alien. Her mother and Aunt Bea preferred the society of women: all girls together—leave the nasty men alone with their brutish ways and their engorged appendages. Men were there to pay the mortgages and mend the fuses when they blew. Send them out onto the path to clean the car and hose the drains, brush the lupins from the grass. And she thought her mother was right after all—that was the difficult part of it. Out of William's arms and beyond his full attention, she was terrified of him, of the power he exercised. She didn't want to love him if it hurt like this; she would be better off despising him.

They spent a quarter of an hour discussing Pamela's problem. She had a friend in Brighton who had promised her some pills if the gin didn't work.

"I could go to Clapham," she said. "But I keep ringing and there's no reply."

She didn't say which one of the group was responsible for her condition.

"Was it George?" asked Ann. She felt it might be. She hadn't met him, but he was the one who had thrown bricks at a policeman and spent two nights in jail.

"I don't want to tell you," said Pamela stubbornly.

She leaned even closer to William, as if Ann was persecuting her. They were moulded in bronze together on the sofa, her chestnut head on his shoulder, his fingers welded to the brown arm of her dressing gown. They were a set piece, a loving statue.

"He ought to be told," persisted Ann, cheeks burning with hostility. It was irresponsible of Pamela to have taken such a risk. She could have gone to a clinic and pretended she was going to get married and been fitted for a Dutch cap. Lots of people did that nowadays. She wondered how they had managed on those communal cushions in the black-painted living room. There weren't any doors, because George had insisted the barriers must be torn down: no one should be shut in or shut out—they must all be free. Pamela had taken him a little too literally.

It occurred to Ann suddenly that she too could have made a dreadful mistake. The shock drained the colour from her face. She looked directly at William, alarm in her eyes. He said, "Better go home and take the pills, Pamela."

"Yes," said Ann. "It would be best."

She wanted her to jump up and leave for Brighton there and then, so that she could be alone with William and be told who she was and to whom she belonged. She had lost her identity. She tore savagely with her teeth at the nail on her thumb. Had she been alone she would have rolled on the floor. She remembered being told that certain animals when injured, paralysed by disease or rifle shot, no longer recognising their own unfeeling limbs, lay down in the shade and gnawed away at paw or foot in an act of self-devouring greed.

William said, "The pills may not work . . . except to give you a bellyache. But if they do, and it starts, you best come back and stay here with us."

His use of the plural seemed to echo in the room —us. The curtains shook at the windows. Downstairs in the hall someone entered from the porch and slammed the door. The foolish Pamela was excluded.

The change in Ann was immediate. She stopped

biting the ends of her fingers and grew calm.

"Yes," she agreed gratefully, generously. "We'll look after you."

He leaned forward then and kissed her on the mouth. The colourless stubble scraped her chin. She wondered how she had ever been afraid of him. It was entirely right and proper that he should be gentle with Pamela and want to comfort her. Who was she to limit his capacity for compassion and goodness? Because he was good and kind, he cared for people and for herself more than anyone. She touched his cheek with her hand, stared deep into his pale eyes and saw her own love reflected there. Between them, dry eyed, sat Pamela with her hands bunched on her stomach.

For almost a week he spent every day with Ann, lying in the unmade bed, talking, putting his record on the gramophone. She waved her arms about in the air and shouted *tum te tum tum tum,* in time to the music, and he watched her, leaning back on the pillows with his hands clasped behind his head. He made her fried-egg sandwiches and she grew not to care about the crumbs or the grease upon the sheets. They spilled tea on the crumpled coverlet, which lay discarded on the floor among the congealed plates and his worn-out raincoat. She loved it being so messy—the way his clothes and his plimsolls lay in a heap on Mrs. Walton's rug. William said they were having an idyll, a pastoral episode, time spent beneath the blue sky of the nursery ceiling.

"But I want it to go on forever," she said. "I don't

want it to be an episode." He told her it was in the nature of an idyll to be episodic: it wasn't meant to last.

Every evening at eight o'clock he left her to go back to his children.

"Sheila has a night job," he said. "I have to read the bairns a story."

She couldn't think what Sheila did in the night and she didn't like to ask. Perhaps she was a char-woman in an office block, or worse, a night cleaner on the railways, taking her mop and her pail along the dark tunnels beneath the city.

When he had gone she bathed and cleaned her teeth and burrowed under the blankets—the head-lights of cars washed across the pink walls as she slept—until he slipped in beside her at four, five in the morning, smelling of soap, enveloping her in goose-pimpled arms, his toes like cold pebbles in the bed, his breath fragrant with cinnamon.

He'd always known he wanted to write: he liked dialogue, the language of the bible, the cadence of rhetoric. It was on account of his father being in the Salvation Army, the hymns he sang as a boy.

"My father's an army man," said Ann. "A Cap-tain."

William went one better and said his Dad was practically a General: he wore a blue uniform, the collar edged with scarlet braid. "Have you never," he asked, "read the *Lives of the Saints?*"

"Never," she was forced to admit.

"The punishment," he said, "the martyrdom. There's glory for you."

It was odd that he liked sacrifice and retribution.

She hadn't thought he was a Puritan.

He had worked as an electrician when he left school, and he married Sheila when he was eighteen. He met her at a dance hall and she was small and dark and refined; she wore a headscarf with wavy lines of yellow and gold. He played football in the street at night; his wife watched him from the doorway and when he kicked the ball close to her, he ran with his eyes on her face, and she turned her head away to hide the pleasure she felt.

"It was a bit of an idyll," he said thoughtlessly, and Ann shifted with pain. He soothed her with caressing words, clapping her back in that now familiar motion of reassurance, saying, "Not like this, my love, not like this, hen."

He'd slept on a truckle bed in the wall when he was a child. She never tired of hearing of his infant self, lying in soiled grey sheets, face turned to the firelight as his mother and father sat by the coals; of the shadows on the brown-leaved wallpaper, stained with damp, the chink in the curtains through which the yellow light shone—a slit of gold—from the lamp on the stone landing at the top of the outside stairs.

"I wish I had known you," she said, conscious that she had lost that part of him, never to return.

Her own childhood by comparison, with its laundered linen and attention to diet, was insipid and valueless. She shared vicariously in that vanished existence he described so vividly—watched him as he slumbered freckle-faced on the truckle bed, stood beside his wife in the doorway of the street.

"Oh, you're beautiful," she cried, surprised at

herself. He was a life-enhancer. She told him she had been much loved as a child, surrounded by warmth and understanding. "My parents are very real people," she said, as if to breathe life into them, and he looked at her and said nothing.

Her mother rang on several occasions—they heard Mrs. Kershaw calling from the stairs. Ann pulled the blankets over her head and refused to budge.

Towards the end of the week, he said she must get up and dress.

"What for?" she asked, loth to leave the bed.

"You just must," he said. "I'll tell you when you're in your clothes."

She did as she was bid, feeling strange and convalescent in her stockings and her skirt.

"Now tell me," she said, coming to him in the kitchen, where he was washing the plates and the cups they had used.

"I'm going to live here," he said. "You know that."

"You are here," she said.

"Aye, I know. But properly . . . my things, my typewriter."

"Oh," she said, thinking of Mrs. Kershaw. They couldn't go on hiding, she supposed. She was due to start work next week. What would Mrs. Kershaw say when she saw William coming down the stairs every morning? "What about my landlady?" she asked. "I don't know how she'll take it." She put her arm round him at the sink and leant her cheek against his broad back.

"Never mind that," he said. "I'm not bothered about her."

He wiped his hands on the tea-towel and loosed her grip on his waist. "My wife is coming round to see you. I couldn't very well forbid it. She's a right to meet you."

"Your wife," she said. "Sheila?"

It was something she hadn't expected; they were divorced, after all. She had thought it would be interesting to have her pointed out in the street, but not here in the flat, with William.

"Not Sheila," he said. "Edna. My wife."

The shock, though monstrous, was not fatal. She stayed leaning against the wall of the kitchen with her hand still on his arm. His face had altered. He was now withdrawn and pompous, with pinched nostrils and lower lip sucked inwards. He spoke very slowly as if to avoid having to repeat any of it again.

"We were married two years ago. She's got a son who's grown up."

"Where is she?" she asked, baffled.

"At home, of course," he said, with some surprise. He turned his back and ran cold water into a glass.

"But why didn't you mention her before . . . in there . . . before?"

He was bulky at the sink, and confident. He stood barefooted and gulped the water noisily.

"We were talking about the past," he said reasonably. "In Glasgow. It had nothing to do with now."

She sat down at the table and curved her shoulders in terror.

"Sit up straight," he told her. "I've not harmed you."

"But you've harmed her," Ann cried. "What about Edna?"

He said sternly, "Let me do the worrying for Edna. It doesn't concern you."

She was dreadfully alarmed that his wife knew he had been coming to see her, spending nights, whole days. "Then why does she have to see me?" she asked, spitefully. "I didn't know you were married."

She wished he would step away from the sink and comfort her. But he stood, arms crossed on his chest, slouching against the draining board.

"I'm her husband," he said. "She has a right to see for herself the sort of person you are. I care about Edna."

Then he did come to her. He patted the top of her head like a schoolmaster with a favourite pupil.

"I'm not good like you," she moaned. "I'd run if I could. I'm scared of what she'll say."

He stroked her neck. He said Edna was a great woman. Ann had no need to be frightened.

"You've lived a bit of a fantasy life, I imagine," he said. "You haven't learned to face things for what they are."

She supposed he was right. She had spent most of her life putting things off, making excuses. However, there had never been any question of Douglas, the married man at the BBC, neglecting to mention he had a wife. He showed everybody photographs of her, and his children. He had a sort of miniature shrine in his car, with them all grouped lovingly at the end of a garden, framed in plastic on the dashboard. She still felt in the back of her mind that William ought to have mentioned Edna. She'd mentioned Gerald.

"There's you and me," said William. "And there's my wife. No getting away from it. That's reality. We'll face it together."

All the same, he didn't stay in the flat to be there when Edna arrived. He said he had to go and see his agent. Ann ran to the bedroom window and heard his footsteps on the gravel, saw his head bobbing above the serrated edge of the privet.

William's wife came an hour later. Outlined behind the frosted glass of the door, she waited for Ann to let her in. She ducked her head and bounced into the small tiled hallway, her grey hair swinging forwards to obscure her face. Ann had difficulty in breathing. She stared at the floor and saw two bright green ballet slippers on Mrs. McClusky's feet.

"Well," said Edna, "this is very distressing, isn't it?"

She had a deep expressive voice and she glided into the sitting room weightlessly and floated about the room. Above her head a cluster of white dots danced on the ceiling. She had a long swanlike neck and bright inquisitive eyes.

"I didn't know," said Ann. "I didn't know about you."

She stood foolishly clasping and unclasping her hands, puzzled by the shifting pattern on the ceiling. Only after several moments, when she moved to the window, did she realise it was the reflection of the sun on a puddle of water on the flat roof outside. Relieved, she looked at Edna's mortal mouth, chapped and brown. Under the aristocratic nose the lips pursed upwards, shaping words. She was saying, "I knew about you two days ago." She wore a black jumper and skirt under a green cloth coat, and she was holding in her hands a small red handkerchief with a white border.

"Honestly," said Ann. "I didn't mean to hurt anybody. I won't see him again."

Edna, who had been prancing about the room looking at the cream walls and the few pictures hung on them, came to a halt on the carpet, with her feet in a ballet position. She turned her head dreamily and rested her chin on her left shoulder. She was graceful and a bit silly. Ann couldn't look at her for fear of smiling. She herself hunched her shoulders and stood loutishly beside the shelf of books.

"William," said Edna, "would like to do what's best for all of us. I know what I want. I'd like to hear what you want."

She's very civilised, thought Ann. Or simple minded. She couldn't bear the sort of introverted conversation they were embarking on. She had, on a very few occasions, been involved in discussion with friends of Mrs. Kershaw. They had asked her the most penetrating questions—it had all been extremely sincere and interesting—but she hadn't been able to discover what it was they needed to know.

"I don't want anything," she said mulishly. "I'm

not in any position to say what I want," she added, thinking maybe she had sounded impolite. "I mean, it's nothing to do with me, is it? It's your husband."

"I don't know how much experience you have of men," began Edna. She was on the move again, darting towards the bunch of carnations long since dead in the glass.

"I'm engaged," said Ann, remembering a convenient fact. "I have a fiancé in America."

"So I've heard. I gather he doesn't count."

Ann felt indignant. "Well, he does," she said. "Really he does." She could see Gerald surrounded by his friends at the farewell party, drinking beer from a cup and growing red in the face.

"Have you told him about William?"

"He's only just left. There hasn't been time." Ann paused, thinking how awful it sounded. Hardly out of the country, hardly landed at Idlewild Airport —and here she was, involved with another lover.

"William," said Edna, "is a beautiful man. A good man."

"Oh, I know," cried Ann. "I know he's good." She could be confident about that. She herself felt more and more wicked as the moments ticked by. She was out of her depth with this dancing woman, the grave theatrical eyes fixed on her, the funny green slippers tripping about the carpet.

"We've known each other for a long time," explained Edna. "I met him when he was living with Gus. We have a good marriage. We care for each other."

Inside, Ann was saying, Don't tell me, I don't

want to know, you have him, I'm going off to Gerald. She watched the red handkerchief in Edna's hands, neatly folded.

"I'm not too old," Edna said, "to have a child. William would like one. You yourself are very young, you have many years ahead of you."

"Yes," said Ann.

"I should like," said Edna, "to keep my husband." The red handkerchief turned in her hands, lost shape and smoothness, twisted like a rag between the long white fingers. All at once her eyes became large and luminous with unshed tears.

"Please," said Ann. "Please forgive me. Don't cry." She took a step forward as if to comfort the older woman. The flecks of light fled from the ceiling. She arrested her hand in the act of patting Edna's back, let it slide instead down the thick wing of grey and crackling hair.

"I'll go away," she said. "To America. As soon as possible. You'll see."

"You can't," said Edna contrarily. "You misunderstand William. If you leave him now at this stage, he'll follow you wherever you go."

"Stage" was an evocative word. There above the footlights stood William, head flung back, holding out his arms imploringly. Ann had never met anyone like Edna before. She thought maybe her mother had tried to be this single-minded, this dogmatic, but time and social milieu had been against her. She couldn't help a small smile of triumph coming to her mouth. She was perfectly willing to escape from William—she wasn't being awkward—

but if he wouldn't let her and Edna wouldn't let her, then she couldn't be blamed.

"Well, what am I to do?" she said belligerently.

"Let him live with you for a little while . . . till his play comes on. Believe me, that's best."

Ann thought she was absurd. Fancy handing your husband over to someone in that way. It came of living in London and mixing with improbable people. That's why William was turning to her; that's what he meant when he spoke about reality. Edna talked about the play in rehearsal, how important it was to William. She said he'd already been commissioned to write a series of half-hour dramas for ITV. "He's earning a vast amount of money. He's very extravagant, very generous." She appeared to be staring at the television set on the window ledge.

"What's his play called?" asked Ann. "The one in rehearsal."

She wondered why Sheila had to go out to clean at night if William was so rich.

"The Truth is a Lie," said Edna. "It's very earthy, very moving." It was about a boy in a tenement room who was different from his parents.

The more Edna talked so proudly of William, the less sympathetic and guilty Ann became. She couldn't understand why this deceived wife didn't rant and rave and call William a despicable beast. No wonder he hadn't mentioned her: she was more like a good friend than a lover—on a par with Gus, who had also been given a ring.

The boy in the tenement went out and played

pool in a hall in the city. Two old men took care of the tables.

Ann didn't know what pool meant.

Edna said, "They love the boy, but they love taking care of the tables more."

While she was talking there were footsteps on the stairs, the rustle of paper, a striking of matches. When the doorbell rang Ann was amazed to see a messenger boy on the landing, holding a large white cake bound with pink ribbon, crowned with flaring candles of red and gold.

"Mrs. McClusky," he said. "Special delivery."

It was Edna's birthday. She said she was forty-two. There were pink roses made from icing sugar and her name written in gold.

"He said I was to expect a surprise," she cried, her face glowing, her long fingers picking and tearing at the circle of small hard roses. She insisted they cut into the cake; she blew out the candles and made a neat incision, extracting a thin sponge slice, layered with cream.

Ann didn't know what to say. It was such an extraordinary thing to do, sending your wife a cake to the flat of another woman. She couldn't for the life of her wish Edna many happy returns of the day.

They sat opposite each other, mouths blocked with the birthday surprise, a faint lingering smell of wax in the room.

*

There were one or two practical details, according to William, that had to be seen to. Ann's job for one.

72

He said she should hand in her notice.

"Oh, I couldn't," she protested. "I couldn't do that."

"Are you fond of your work then? Is it absorbing to you?"

"No," she admitted. "I wouldn't say that."

"Right," he said. "Chuck it in. There's no virtue in working if you don't have to. I've enough money for us all."

Then there was the question of who should tell Mrs. Kershaw he had moved into the flat.

"I'll do it," he said. "I'm sure she's a reasonable kind of woman."

He was downstairs for two hours. Ann suffered lest he was being persuaded not to stay. She knew William would then insist they should move somewhere else—and what would her mother think about that? She hadn't had the courage to mention William yet, but she was working up to it. Perhaps Mrs. Kershaw knew Edna—they moved in the same sort of circles. Perhaps she was telling William to go back to his wife, that she didn't approve of immorality. It wasn't very likely and Ann knew it, but half of her wanted someone, somewhere, to make a decision for her so she wouldn't have to feel guilty. She hadn't told William what Edna had said about having children, about wanting to keep him. He hadn't asked. He just wanted to know how her face had looked when the cake arrived. Mrs. Kershaw raised no objections. She even gave William an extra key.

"She's a great woman," he said, lying down on the sofa and kicking off his shoes. "Who's the chap she lives with?"

"Roddy," Ann said. "Was he there? Did you meet him?"

"No," he said. "He wasn't in."

"Didn't she mind at all? Wasn't she worried about my mother finding out?"

"Aye, she mentioned your mother. She said you were grown-up now."

As if that had anything to do with it. "People are funny," she mused. "In London, they don't seem to object to anything."

"A woman like that," he said. "It would be a strange thing if she raised objections."

Ann felt he disapproved of Mrs. Kershaw, though she had offered to lend him her bicycle whenever he wanted.

They mustn't, William said, go on staying in bed all the time, however much he wished to. There were rehearsals he ought to be attending, discussions with his agent.

"Yes," said Ann, nodding her head violently in agreement. "You're right."

But it was difficult planning to get up at a reasonable hour when he came home at four in the morning. There was the love-making, the egg sandwiches. Then he would sing to her the folk songs he had learnt in the wardrobe with Gus. He taught her his father's favourite hymn, "The Sea of Love is Rolling In." There were two lines in particular she never tired of hearing, because they rhymed so well and she could get the tune immediately, not like the cello concerto he still played from time to time on the gramophone.

If I perceive
What I believe—

She would join in the chorus—

It's rolling in,
It's rolling in . . .

holding him in her arms and rocking from side to
side in the bed—

The sea of love is rolling in . . .

The man in the flat next door hurled himself against
the wall and groaned audibly. During the day she
crept down the stairs like a mouse to collect her
mother's letter, in fear and trembling lest she met
him. She didn't bloom like it said in the library
books; the smudges of fatigue under her eyes only
served to accentuate the thinness of her face.

Finally, William made her write to Gerald. She
remembered her promise to Edna, the fact that William was on loan, that she had to give him back. Her
tongue clove to the roof of her mouth at the memory of the birthday cake. She swallowed and thought
it unfair that she had to give up a husband and a
home in America. If she was going to be unhappy,
doomed to spend the rest of her life without William, then she might as well have the next best
thing. William said she was a daft wee hen. He was
never going back to Edna. He loved only her. They
would grow old together by the fire.

"We haven't got one," she said, looking at the

blocked-in grate and the central-heating pipes circling the room.

She had already descended into the painful habit, whenever he mentioned meeting some woman or other, of asking him had he been to bed with her. He always said he had. It was very honest but, for someone who had been struck by the glory of the lives of the saints, it was contradictory. Resentfully she wrote the letter he dictated—

My dear Gerald,
    I don't want to hurt you. I would avoid inflicting pain if I could. I have to be truthful. I have fallen in love with someone else—

"He'll think it's a bit sudden," she said. "I was always telling him I hadn't known him long enough to be sure of my feelings."

"Well then," said William. "It won't come as a shock." And he stroked her breast and urged her to finish the letter. It was two pages long and quite unlike her own style of correspondence.

She said, "Isn't it a bit emotional?"

"It's meant to be," he said. "You're turning the poor bugger down."

He told her they must post it right away.

They both appeared pale and languid in the street. She imagined he must have lost weight; his raincoat hung on him, the plimsolls flapped on his bare feet. They walked hand in hand up the hill to the stationers. It was only the second time she had been in the open air with him, unless she could count the moments they had leaned out of the bedroom window to watch the dawn. When they had bought the air-mail envelopes, she realised they couldn't send the letter. There was no address, as yet.

"I feel so weak," she said. "We ought to buy some food." She had eaten nothing in six days save the portion of Edna's cake, and the fried-egg sand-wiches.

"Loving you," he said. "I don't feel the need for food."

She thought how romantic it was that he was go-ing without nourishment because of her. And yet he looked so well on it. It was a compliment to the quality of her love. She knew what she should buy —butter, bread, cheese—but apart from a bottle of H.P. sauce that William wanted, she couldn't con-centrate. He was walking between the shelves with her, nibbling the corner of her mouth, pushing his hand through the opening of her coat.

She wandered up and down the shop, undecid-edly. Eventually, without buying anything more, they walked out into the street, up the road to the Heath. There was pale sunlight. The glass glittered as it bent in the wind. They lay huddled under the drooping trees and touched each other with cold hands. She liked being indoors better; outside she had to keep asking him what he had said, what he meant. His voice was high and dragged away by the wind. He had found in the pocket of his coat a scarf in different bands of blue. He wound it round his neck. She wondered who had knitted it—his mother or one of those women he had continually met in the past. He told her the breed of ducks on the pond, the name for the clouds swelling in the sky, the particular metal on the green dome of the church beyond the bridge. He knew everything—trees, plants, seasons and conditions—he talked about racehorses, painters, the excellence of footballers. There was no end to the detail of his knowledge.

"Arkle," she said. "Why is he so different? This Arkle."

He explained that once in a generation a foal was thrown that was superior to any that had gone before. A miracle. That was Arkle.

"What about Samuel Palmer," she said. "Why is he so nice?"

He told her about a self-portrait, the smear of flake white in the pupil of the left eye. "What he did," he said, "was to paint his face one side at a time. It explains the rustic quality, lop-sided, the mouth, the squashed-down hair."

"What hair?" she wanted to know.

"His hair," he said. "Like as if he had gone into the yard and put his head under the pump."

"Is that all he did," said Ann. "Self-portraits?"

"He painted sheep under the moon."

"And Dennis Law?" she asked. "What's so special about him?" She was becoming irritated by all these people who were so close to him.

"Ah," he said. "He's a great man. The greatest of them all." He went into a description that she couldn't follow, involving muscles in the leg, turns of speed on the pitch, the way a ball was kicked into the net.

"Oh, a footballer," she said, scornfully. He

looked at her as if she was simple.

He spoke then of his father in Glasgow, his blue uniform, the manner in which he polished his trumpet with a bit of rag and spat into the fire.

She liked hearing about his father. She thought maybe he was a little like William to look at. He was a saver of souls. What a friend he had in Jesus! She shivered with the cold under the October sky and William said he would buy her a fur coat of beaver lamb.

"I'll get you a grey woollen dress with a white collar," he promised. "Would you like that, my beauty?"

"Yes," she said submissively.

They were too frail to walk home. He signalled a taxi in Heath Street and they sat leaning against each other with the sauce bottle balanced on his knee. On Haverstock Hill the taxi was slowed by a line of traffic at a school crossing. Ann saw a woman on the pavement with bushy black hair. She wore a strange expression of excitement and curiosity as she trotted beside the crawling taxi.

"Concentrate wholly on me," said William. He pulled Ann to him and began to kiss her neck. He wasn't tired any more. He was urgent and amorous. He pushed her to the floor of the moving vehicle as it swung round the corner and down the hill. He lay on top of her. His nails hurt her thigh; her head was flung against the door. Suddenly there was a jolt and her foot flew upwards at the impact. Her shoe came off.

"Now," said William. "Now."

She was covered in dust. She was aware of argumentative voices—the sound of car horns. The branches of a tree rocked outside the window. William's door opened. He raised himself on to his knees. There was a circle of men about the hood of the taxi. The driver was in the road thumping a small, expensively dressed man on the shoulder. "Fuck off," he was shouting. "Fuck off in your plastic gondolier, back to the promised land." They moved backwards and forwards, retreating and advancing; they circled one another, like dancers.

The cars had been involved in some sort of collision. The driver said you could see by the state of his passengers that it had been fucking serious. People came to the window and peered in at Ann. She wiped at her coat with her fingers, searched for her shoe. William's trousers were undone. The abused man climbed back into his car and drove away in a cloud of exhaust fumes. The leaves leapt from the gutter and bowled down the brow of the hill. The cab driver apologised for the rough journey. He said his name was Lionel. Ann held the sauce bottle and lay with her head in William's lap. All the way home he and Lionel kept up a spirited conversation about bloody Yids.

"Are you prejudiced?" asked Ann, and William shook her by the shoulder and said he was anything anyone wanted him to be.

At eight o'clock that night he left, as usual, to read his children a story. He rode the hill now on Mrs. Kershaw's bicycle, back bent under the street lamps, trousers flapping as he pedalled upwards.

She went trembling to the telephone in the hall. She wanted to talk to her mother.

"Mummy," she said, whispering in case Roddy heard. "I'm in such a muddle."

"Oh yes. And what about, pray?"

The voice was hostile but Ann was undeterred. Exhaustion and emotion had blurred her sense of judgment.

"I've met someone. I really am in love."

"Oh indeed. And what does he do?"

"He's a writer."

"A writer. What school did he go to?"

"I don't know, Mummy. He's very rich. Oh Mummy, he's married."

"It's every woman for herself," said Mrs. Walton.

"But his wife?" Ann could see Edna in a come-dancing mood, gliding about her home, devoid of husband. "It's all wrong, isn't it?" she asked, wanting confirmation.

"What does his father do?"

"He's a General, Mummy, in—"

But Mrs. Walton was over the moon with delight. A General. How pleased Captain Walton would be.

It was too late to mention the brass band playing in the gutter—the sea of love was rolling in.

"I'll come down and meet him," Mrs. Walton threatened. "Just say the word."

"Wait," said Ann. "Not yet. Wait."

She cursed herself for having told her mother about William. From then on she lived in constant fear of that step on the stair, the veiled hat with the primroses stiffly waving, emerging from the taxi, the gloved hand extended to greet the General's son.

3

Pamela sent a telegram to say she was arriving from Brighton on the midday train. William had an appointment with a man who was going to help him with his income tax. Ann had intended to go with him, but in the circumstances she said she would stay behind and wait for Pamela.

"Don't fret yourself," said William. "I'll fetch her in a taxi from the station."

He didn't say why Ann couldn't go too—perhaps it was because he might miss Pamela at the station. He appeared from the bedroom wearing a brown Ivy League suit and a pale green shirt with button-down collar.

"You do look smart," said Ann. She supposed he had collected it from Edna's some time during the week. She didn't like to ask if he saw Edna at all—sometimes there were fairly mysterious telephone conversations that made her go into the bathroom and run the taps for fear he would think she had been eavesdropping on the landing. In certain ways she sensed he was like her father, private and reserved.

His desk and typewriter were now installed in the living room. Her own books had gone from the two shelves above the blocked-in grate, replaced by a row of dictionaries and several volumes of Shakespearean plays. He said he could just pile his books on the floor, but she thought it looked untidy; so she took down the few volumes of poetry, her collection of detective stories, the miscellaneous novels she possessed, and stacked them neatly under the bed. She didn't mind in the least.

When he had gone a woman phoned and asked to speak to him.

"He's out," Ann said. "He's had to meet someone."

"Oh, he's left, has he?" said the woman.

"Can I take a message?" asked Ann politely, but the woman hung up.

When William returned with Pamela, they climbed the stairs slowly. He supported her round the waist. He moved the sofa against the wall and covered her with blankets. She still shivered. She'd taken the pills as directed, and she said she was in pain. Like a period, only much worse. Agony. William made her several cups of strong tea and went downstairs to borrow sugar from Mrs. Kershaw.

"How do you feel?" said Ann, at a loss.

"Awful," Pamela said. She wore a perky little smile and there was moisture on her forehead. The straight eyebrows met in the centre above eyes round and brown as a doll's.

"We best get her a doctor," said William.

"Wait," Pamela said. Like Ann, she felt in these circumstances it would be prudent to avoid calling a doctor. It was illegal, wasn't it, to take pills for such a purpose?

At five o'clock she sat up and attempted to stand on the carpet. A thin trickle of blood ran down the inside of her leg and splashed her heel. She was sick onto her bare toes before they could fetch a bowl. William washed her feet in warm water and dried them tenderly. He sang "The Green Oak Tree" to her. She lay flat on her back with her arm flung over her eyes and moaned slightly. Tears ran from the crook of her elbow and dripped on to her pointed chin. She was still bleeding at eight o'clock when William went to phone the ambulance.

"You can't go downstairs on a stretcher," said Ann. "Can't you stand up at all?"

"I'll try," Pamela said weakly. "But I feel awful."

She appeared to lose consciousness; she lay completely still and lifeless. Ann ran to the top of the stairs to call William. She could hear him on the phone. "I'll maybe drop by later," she heard him say. "I'm a bit caught up."

"William," called Ann in terror. "Come quick."

He said she was only faint from loss of blood. He had seen this kind of thing before. They would doubtless give her a blood transfusion.

"Where have you seen this kind of thing before?" asked Ann.

"Here and there," he replied. "Do you know her blood group?"

"No," said Ann, "I don't."

She wrung her hands in misery and hoped Pamela wouldn't die.

"Who were you talking to?" she asked William, looking at her cousin's waxen cheeks and the dark hair limp with perspiration.

"The hospital," he said. "They'll be along in a moment."

He carried Pamela downstairs in his arms. Ann followed with Pamela's toothbrush and some magazines. The ambulance men laid her on a stretcher in the hall, folded and packed her neatly in a bright red blanket that glowed against the dull green carpet. She looked like an exotic parcel. She was carried over the gravel, pathetically mewing as she swung gently between the stretcher bearers. William and Ann sat silently inside the dim interior of the van. William leant his elbows on his knees and watched the pale face, luminous above the cheerful rug.

How far we have travelled, thought Ann, though it was not the distance to the hospital she was contemplating, but more specifically her attitude to life, her abandonment of standards. In ten days she had encouraged adultery, committed a breach of promise, given up her job, abetted an abortion. She had not been aware, throughout these happenings, of any unease or distress. She had become like one of those insect specimens under glass, sucked dry of her old internal organs, pumped full and firm with an unknown preservative. She was transfixed by William. I don't mind, she thought, as the ambulance bounced down the ramp to the hospital. Pamela was conscious now. She made a little moan of protest as she was rolled from the stretcher on to the high bed in a small emergency room off Main Reception.

"I could kill George," said Ann, but it didn't help anyone.

After some moments, a Sister came and took the patient's name and that of her doctor in Brighton.

"Phelps," said Ann, lying in case Pamela's mother was informed. "Arnold Phelps, The Parade, Brighton." She thought it was rather quick and clever. "No," she said, "I don't know her blood group."

When the Sister had gone she told William it wasn't true. "Didn't I do well?" she said.

The door into the emergency room was open. They could see Pamela under the raspberry blanket —the tip of her nose, a curve of lip.

"That's my girl," said William, smiling; but Ann wasn't sure whom he meant. He was looking at Pamela. Don't be silly, she told herself, and she shook her head irritably and reached for his hand. He took it at once and his face above the green shirt was broad and solemn. The blue eyes held love. He arched his pale brows and stared at her. His hand lay over hers, white and plump. If men were supposed to be beautiful—if it wasn't effeminate—then that was what he was, beautiful.

"It won't ever be like that for us," she said. "Will it? You won't make me take pills, will you?"

She knew he wouldn't, but it was nice to ask because the answer was so obvious.

"Never," he said, and he did mean it. He pushed her down on to the waiting-room bench, scattering the *Woman's Own* and the *Country Life*, sending them sliding across the polished floor, with his bullet head trapping a section of her hair, his hands beneath her coat pushing her skirt up about her hips. Nobody but them in Reception, the clock ticking on the wall, the gleaming corridors stretching beyond the swing doors, the plastic cushions sticking to her bottom, an edge of crimson blanket like blood against the white wall. She thought she knew now why William behaved as he did. He couldn't compromise or wait for the right moment or the right place; he loved her so much. He wanted to show her —in this building, silent as a church and sanctified with disinfectant—the discrepancy between one act of love and another. Not quite silent: there was the sound of rubber-soled shoes, an indignant cry— Sister with her safety pin and her watch, her little white hat like knickers on her head—shaking William disgustedly by the shoulder, ordering them out, calling them names, saying she would send for the police.

"I'm not ashamed," said Ann defiantly, once she was in the street and away from censure. "I don't care."

"No," said William. "You're a great little learner." And he took her by the arm and ran her up the alley into Belsize Park, cuddling her like a friend in the warm underground train, proud of her.

Afterwards, though, Ann was dismayed by her behaviour. Poor Pamela, losing her piece of baby in the clinical room. What a time to affirm that she herself was loved and in no such danger. "What a dreadful thing to happen," she said, wide-eyed in the dark. She was thinking of herself lying on the bench with her suspenders showing.

"Pamela will be all right," William said; and he didn't bother to go and read his children a story, but fell asleep with his face crumpled against her stomach and the sheets flung back like a ripped-open envelope.

*

The next evening, at visiting time, Ann wouldn't go to the hospital.

"I'm sorry," she said. "I just can't do it."

She didn't like William going without her, but equally she couldn't face that Sister in Reception. Fretting, she let him walk out of the flat with a bunch of anemones and four oranges.

She read again the letter that had arrived from Gerald earlier in the day. William had torn the University address from the top of the page and made her copy it onto the airmail envelope containing her farewell letter to Gerald; he had taken it with him when he went out to buy the posy and the fruit for Pamela. Gerald wrote that he had settled in and made friends with a young couple who rented a cabin at weekends in the mountains. He didn't say where. It disturbed her, the whole tone of the letter. Even the bit about longing to hold her in his arms didn't reassure her, coming as it did after a long paragraph about seeing two bears standing in the driven snow. He sounded so happy. She had been mortified to let William read it. He sounded as if he was perpetually enjoying himself and on some sort of Outward Bound course, instead of working diligently as a lecturer and saving for their future. Of course, there was to be no future now, but he hadn't known that when he wrote to her. Her own letter, telling him she loved another, would hardly break his stride, would not perceptibly narrow the contour of his eye as he squinted down the barrel of his gun. She would leave no imprint on the virgin snow.

She went downstairs to talk to Mrs. Kershaw and met Roddy in the hall. He was on his hands and knees searching for something. There was no furniture to look under, so his position was remarkable.

"Have you seen a parcel?" he demanded. "A big parcel in brown paper with an Irish postmark?"

"No," she said. "When did you last see it?"

"I've never seen it," said Roddy.

He wore a judo outfit of white canvas, the trousers halfway up his legs, his feet bare.

Mrs. Kershaw was painting a small grey pot dark brown. Her manner, though not unfriendly, was not the same as previously. She was both more relaxed and less courteous. There was a young man with golden hair sitting in a corner of the room with both hands covering his face. She didn't tell Ann to sit down, nor did she call her "Dear." She neglected to introduce her to the young man.

"I had a letter from Gerald," Ann said. "He seems fine." She stood by the table that was covered with newspapers and wished she had stayed upstairs.

"Good," said Mrs. Kershaw. She didn't ask what Ann intended to do about her fiancé in America. She bit her lip in concentration and brushed paint onto the earthenware pot. The room was full of artistic objects—pottery and paintings and bits of dried twigs and pieces of rock. Against the window wall was a whole dead tree, its blackened branches curling upwards to the ceiling. Ann couldn't help thinking it was fortunate Mrs. Kershaw didn't own a dog. How Mrs. Walton would have hated the untidiness, the sense of freedom. She wondered if she too ought to start making things, now that she no longer had a job. But she had never been any good at drawing and she supposed it was a little late to start now. Art was surely like learning the violin: the fingers stiffened up if you didn't begin when you were a child.

"Has William gone out again?" asked Mrs. Kershaw.

There was the faintest hint of accusation. Perhaps she was annoyed that William was forever taking her bicycle.

"Yes," said Ann, though she couldn't explain about Pamela.

Roddy came in and threw books and cushions from off the sofa.

"It's not here," said Mrs. Kershaw. "I've looked."

The young man raised his head and Ann was concerned to see he had been crying and was continuing to do so. She didn't want to stare, but it was like seeing a cripple in the street and not being able to look anywhere else. Neither Mrs. Kershaw nor Roddy took any notice. The phone rang in the hall.

"I'll answer it," said Ann in relief, and she picked up the receiver and heard Edna say, "May I speak to William McClusky."

"He's not in," said Ann. She was pleased to hear

91

Edna's voice. They had a lot in common—she felt they were almost friends.

"It's gone eight," said Edna. "I wondered what had happened to him."

"He had to visit someone . . . a relative of mine."

"But it's the second night in succession. Dinner will be spoilt." The voice was carefully modulated but offended. Ann could tell, because of the training with her mother.

"Oh, how inconsiderate," she said. "I'm terribly sorry."

"You're not to blame," said Edna carefully. She hoped Ann was well. She asked her to tell William she had rung.

"Oh, I will," said Ann.

Only when she had replaced the receiver did she start to tremble. She was so shaken she didn't bother to say goodnight to Mrs. Kershaw. She ran upstairs and walked about the living room with pounding heart. It was the fact that William had been eating dinners that registered most clearly. Lamb, vegetables and gravy, thick soups. Her mouth watered and her nostrils quivered at the imaginary smells of roasting meat. She saw in full colour a crisp roll smeared with salted butter, the leaves of a cabbage, steaming, sprinkled with black pepper. Not until these visions had subsided, a series of photographs in a cookery book, each item displayed on tasteful crockery, was she aware of other implications. He hadn't been reading stories to his children after all. He had been at Edna's. Had he left after his meal and pedalled on his borrowed bicycle to Sheila's? Did people start work at that time of night? She had no idea where Sheila lived. Was it an hour away, downhill, or round the corner? She was tormented by geographical details, map references, grid systems. She stared out into the darkness of the back garden and tried to visualise the position of the houses he visited, the dimensions of the rooms he sat in. Like a small red star, the rear light on the mudguard of his cycle trailed across the city. Did he eat food with his wives, either of them, and then lie down in a bed? Could men do that? He didn't seem tired when he returned. Gerald had, on several occasions, done it twice, and complained that she was killing him. And he hadn't been cycling anywhere. She just didn't know enough about men. Her mother said they were brutes, self-absorbed and secretive. But William wasn't like that: he was open and he loved her and he had forced her to meet his wife. It was incomprehensible to her. She dug the pads of her fingers into the corner of her eyes and moaned for her mother. She prowled about the circumference of the room and waited for him to return.

When he did, a little after four, she ran to the door as he let himself in.

"What the hell have you been doing?" she asked.

She wrapped her thin arms about herself for fear her hands would fly out and strike him. She stood in the tiled hallway and heard her voice strained and unloving. He handed her two brown leaves of sycamore; she flung them to the floor and ground them with her heel. They broke up like bits of burnt pa-

93

per; she remembered her mother in the fluffy bed-jacket, tossing the conciliatory carnations from the bed.

"Edna rang," he said. "Is that what's upset you?"

He looked tired. Maybe it was only the light bulb casting shadows on his face, but there were hollows she hadn't seen before and the delicate skin under his eyes was bruised almost to the cheekbones.

"What did you tell lies for?" she said bitterly. Though she knew, because she had always told lies —been forced to, since a child. It was other people expecting too much.

"It wasn't a lie," he said. "Will you listen to me."

He avoided the bedroom. He sat her shivering on the sofa, her white nightdress soiled with egg at the hem. She dug her toes into the cushions for warmth and glared at him.

"I never said," he began, "that I wasn't seeing my wife. I never lied about that."

He didn't seem to realise it was the number of his wives that was causing the confusion.

"Maybe I kept from you how much I saw of her. I'll give you that."

He paced the room, turning like a soldier at the window and marching to the door.

"I have been reading the children a story at night. Not every night, I grant you, or all night. But I have been to see them."

"How many times?" she said tearfully, as if that would make it better.

"Several times. I haven't been counting. But Edna needs to look after me. I give her money for the housekeeping . . . she doesn't want to be done out of cooking for me. Who am I to deny her that?"

He bent his head humbly. There was a flaw in his argument, she knew, but she couldn't put it into words. He'd denied Edna everything else; it didn't seem particularly cruel to tell her he didn't want any food.

"But you can't be eating till four o'clock in the morning," she cried.

"No," he said, with the trace of a smile. "No, that's not possible."

Then there was silence. He constantly forced her to make readjustments; she had only to get used to one set of circumstances and he faced her with others. He wouldn't tell her what he did after he ate; he waited to see if she was brave enough to ask. She wasn't. "Don't you want to know how Pamela is?" he asked.

"How is she?" She forced her face to show concern; she raised her eyebrows eagerly as if it was the only subject on her mind.

"She's on the mend. There was a doctor who tried to get out of her what she'd done to bring it on. She didn't tell him. She'll be home in a day or two. I thought we might go away somewhere, the three of us, when she's stronger."

"That's lovely," said Ann.

But it wasn't. It was one more complication. What was he doing visiting her cousin, carrying her down the stairs, making plans to take her on holiday? I loathe Pamela, she wanted to shout; she smashed my sand castles with her spade, she held my head under the sea. "I'm sorry," she said. "I just feel something's not quite right somewhere. I'm not

95

clever enough to know what, but I feel it." And, inspired, she beat the breast of her white nightdress with her fist.

He was slumped on the sofa now, worn out. He yawned and yawned, exactly like a cat, she thought, the tip of his pink tongue on the edge of his teeth and his eyes opening and shutting.

"There's nothing wrong," he said. "It's just life putting the boot in."

It was one of his sayings, learnt from Gus. He was holding her bare right foot among the cushions, his fingers uncurling the stubborn snail of her little toe.

"I've never," he said, "felt like this about anyone. You'll just have to believe me. I do have compartments to my life, I can't deny that, but I've never loved anyone like this before." He looked at her smooth face, the small wanton mouth, the gullible eyes that watched him greedily.

He was telling the truth. His voice was rough with emotion, unless it was the strain of his multiple yawns—and though she didn't like or understand what he meant by compartments, she did know he was being sincere.

"It's all right," she said. "I do believe you."

They lay on the sofa with the daylight beginning to grow outside the window, his arm loosely about her. It was dreadfully sad and yet beautiful. There wasn't anything, actually, you could do with love once you'd talked about it. After it had been mentioned, it hung like smoke in the air and drifted this way and that. What kind of compartments did he mean—airtight ones or the sort on railway trains? Was she locked away on her own, or was he in the compartment with her? His desk was here, his best suit, his razor in the bathroom. Even if he had gone to bed with his wife, did it matter? Edna wasn't beautiful or even young: she was forty-two and grey-haired and life was putting the boot in. You couldn't hope to be all things to one person at all times. It made her feel important and extended, having come to such a conclusion. She hadn't known how philosophical she could be. It was something in him that brought out the best in her.

"Let's not think about it too much," she said cunningly. "Let's just go to sleep and wake up together."

*

He didn't go and see Edna or the children for several days. Once he went out on his bicycle to visit Gus. From the window Ann saw him on the pavement pushing a brown paper parcel inside his raincoat. He'd said he was taking some shirts to Gus, who was unemployed at the moment. It was sensible to put the parcel against his heart: otherwise he wouldn't be able to steer properly.

"Don't be long," she called, and he blew her a kiss. He was back within the hour.

Pamela was discharged from hospital and Ann took care of her. Having survived William's deceit, she felt she was now older and more capable of love. She brushed Pamela's hair, made her toast and boiled egg, bought her a new flannel—bright purple—from John Barnes. She made little jokes to take Pamela's mind off her recent ordeal—about home, their mothers' combined snobbery. She even laughed about her father in the greenhouse, all those years ago.

"Poor man," said Pamela, "I don't think they ever do it. Any of our parents."

"It's probably all that saluting and standing to attention," Ann said. "He's probably done himself an injury." And she shrieked with laughter, falling backwards onto the sofa, kicking her heels in the air.

"You have changed," said Pamela, watching her from the divan, propped up on cushions and the foot of the bed raised up on William's dictionaries.

In the evening they played rummy round the sofa, a penny a hundred. Ann, used to playing with her mother, was astonished by William's lack of competition. Sometimes he lost on purpose. Now and then he would jump up from the floor and scribble something down on a piece of paper at his desk. His broad back blotted out the light. He showed Ann his cards and asked her what she wanted him to throw away. "Stop it," she said. "Play properly."

He had altered the room, rearranged the furniture, hung pictures on the wall of Samuel Palmer and Dennis Law. He had pushed into a cupboard the electric kettle that had stood on the window ledge, the electric clock her mother had given her for her eighteenth birthday. "I hate gadgets," he had said. "I hate all those wires." He had moved the lamp to the corner of the room. They sat, the three of them, in near darkness, peering at the cards. Pamela's slippers kept falling off. She bent downwards from the sofa to retrieve them, and the turkish necklace slithered between her breasts, the coins jangling as she moved.

Ann was embarrassed at night by the violence of William's love-making—she was sure Pamela must hear them. Brutally he twisted her arms behind her back and held her head still, with his teeth in the soft lobe of her ear. It was exciting, but she was sure they made an awful noise. She imagined the man next door, resigned to the hymn singing and the laughter, putting his ear to the wall and waiting with renewed hope for them to murder one another. "Rubbish," said William, "He's bought ear plugs by now, or moved out."

In the mornings she opened wide the windows to air the sheets, helped Pamela from the sofa and tucked her into the double bed, to be more comfortable.

"Shall I try to get George to come?" she asked.

She wasn't hostile to George any more. She could see he had merely placed Pamela in a compartment. It wasn't his fault if someone had pulled the communication cord and hurled everyone out onto the platform.

"No," said Pamela. "Leave it. I'll phone soon."

Ann, determined to take Edna's place, shopped every morning on the Finchley Road. She wouldn't take money from William; she insisted on drawing on her savings at the bank. On the third day, when she came in from buying a chicken, she was upset to find William, dressed only in a shirt, on the bed with Pamela. He was reading her his play.

"You've never read it to me," cried Ann, sick with jealousy.

He leapt up at once and put on his trousers and came through to her in the kitchen.

"Sit down," he said. "Leave that alone and look at my play."

He put the script in front of her. She wouldn't open it.

"You shouldn't do that," she whispered. "It's not right."

"What isn't?" he said.

"Lying on our bed, with her. Without your clothes."

"Jesus," he said, "Don't be so bloody narrow. I'm like a brother to her."

Being an only child, she was in no position to judge. Sulkily she turned the foolscap sheets. There were at least two pages devoted to three old men talking about a billiard table. They kept repeating the same sentences.

"Are they important?" she asked. "The old men?"

"Yes and no," he said. "Anyone who makes a statement is important to the structure. Just some are more important than others."

"Oh," she said.

She read—

1st Old Man: I don't like ma' table having dust on it.

2nd Old Man: You dinna like that!

3rd Old Man: That's wha' he said.

1st Old Man: I know wha' I said.

3rd Old Man: It's not your table that has the dust on it.

2nd Old Man: You dinna like that!

3rd Old Man: That's wha' he said.

1st Old Man: I know wha' I said.

3rd Old Man: It's not your table that has the dust on it.

2nd Old Man: Nor mine, either.

1st Old Man: Well it's ma' dust. That's for sure.

2nd Old Man: For twenty years he's cleaned tha' table. Let him have his table.

1st Old Man: Let him get rid of his bloody dust then.

"It's lovely," said Ann, putting down the script. "You've captured exactly the way old men talk."

"You haven't finished it."

"I want to read it when I'm on my own. I want to take time to read it."

She laid it on the surface of his desk and made coffee for the three of them. Secretly she felt it was rubbish. All that talk about dust. She wanted to think it was lovely—she would have done, if he hadn't been reading it to Pamela on the bed. When they were drinking their coffee he said he was going to get brochures from a travel agency. He thought they should all go to Spain. Pamela rubbed her forehead with her hand as if she had a headache. He and Gus had gone to Barcelona three years ago and the sun would do Pamela good.

"But it's winter," said Ann. "It's winter in Spain."

"But mild," he said. "Not like here."

When he had gone, Ann sat on the window sill

and told Pamela that if she didn't mind she felt it would be best if she went home, or to stay with George in Clapham. She looked down at the gravel path, at the clump of withered wallflowers by the dustbins.

"I don't want to be unkind," she said. "But it is awkward. The way he includes you, brings you trays to the bed, wants you to come with us on holiday. We've other problems—his wives, for instance."

Pamela, surprisingly, knew about that. William had told her when he visited her in the hospital.

"He's not an ordinary man," Pamela said, lying back on the pillow. "You don't want to expect normality from him. He's an artist, after all."

"I know," said Ann, annoyed that it had occurred to Pamela first.

"I just don't want you to come on holiday with us. You do see why, don't you?"

"Perfectly," said Pamela. "I didn't intend to, anyway." She started to peel an orange, tugging at it with her teeth.

"Do you think I'm very unkind?" asked Ann. "I'm trying to be honest."

The invalid said nothing; juice trickled from her stubborn lips. Later she went down into the hall to make a phone call. She shuffled back up the stairs with her dressing gown trailing behind her.

"He says I can come tomorrow," she said.

*

Ann wanted to go in the taxi with her and see her safely to the door. After all, Pamela had lost a lot of blood and was still weak, or pretending to be. She moved wearily about the flat collecting her belongings, the necklace jingling on her pale neck. But she preferred to go alone.

"George wouldn't care for it," she said. "He'll think you've come to shout at him."

Willian had said goodbye to her earlier, before going to have lunch with the producer of his play. He didn't ask why Pamela had decided to move out so suddenly. The brochures he had brought from the travel agency lay on the television set, gaudy with setting suns and Moorish architecture. He shook hands formally with Pamela. He was wearing a black jacket Ann hadn't seen before, and grey trousers. His tie, which was mauve, looked as if it was made of brushed velvet. The wardrobe in the pink bedroom was bursting with his elegant clothes, his laundered shirts. He said he hoped Pamela would find everything all right in Clapham.

"Thank you," said Pamela demurely. "You've been very kind." She wouldn't, Ann noticed, look William in the eye.

At four o'clock Ann telephoned George's house. She had found the number in an address book Pamela had left on the bathroom shelf. A man answered who said his name was Edward. George had left last week for Cornwall.

"I'm Pamela's cousin," said Ann.

He hadn't the faintest idea at first who Pamela was. After some prompting he conceded that she might be a girl belonging to George.

"With fair hair?" he said.

"No, she's dark."

"Face like a Victorian doll," he said. "Is that the one?"

But he hadn't seen her recently. Nor had anyone called at the house that afternoon. He'd have known anyway, because George had taken the bolt off the front door before he left.

*

Ann was late for her period. She knew the reason for it, but she didn't want to admit it. Lately she wasn't sure she knew how to take care of herself, let alone a child. She had bad dreams about William leaving on ships and aeroplanes, standing at rails and on gangplanks, waving, with a shadowy woman at his side.

"It could be," she told William, "that I'm run down. Lack of sleep, worry over Pamela, that sort of thing."

She had read somewhere that, in the concentration camps, the women had stopped menstruating through lack of food.

"Rubbish," said William. "You're pregnant."

He seemed pleased, and yet he never mentioned marriage. She would have liked to contact Pamela to discuss symptoms and things with her, but she didn't dare admit to William that Pamela had never arrived in Clapham. Nor did she want to phone Brighton to see if she was at home. What would she say if Aunt Bea said she understood Pamela was staying with her?

William insisted on taking her to a surgery he knew. Only when they were in the waiting room did

he tell her this particular doctor took care of Edna
and Sheila and the children. The doctor made William stay outside while he questioned her. William
didn't want to go; he would have sat quite proudly
at her side and held her hand.

She lay clammily under the cotton sheet, her face
pink and aloof. The doctor had gold cuff-links and
a gold tie pin. He wore rubber gloves as if he were
going to do the washing-up, and he smelled of tal-
cum powder. He said it was far too early to tell. He
made a slight examination of her and explained he
didn't want to probe too much as he presumed she
wanted the baby, and at this stage it was as well to
leave things alone.

"Oh yes," she said. "I want it."

She would have liked to ask him how long he had
known William and Edna and Sheila. Did he think
William intended to marry her? But there was
hardly the opportunity. She was relieved not to be
told she was definitely pregnant.

William wanted to go out and buy a pram at John
Barnes. Ann said there was nowhere to put it and
they ought to wait at least till her condition was
confirmed. In the hall downstairs, there was already
installed an enormous wardrobe with brass handles,
belonging to William. Roddy had asked twice for its
removal, but William said he would shift it when
Mrs. Kershaw objected, not before. When he was
out Ann tiptoed downstairs and looked inside.
There were suits and jackets, an overcoat of dark
blue, a new silk dressing gown. Polished shoes,
brown and black, and suede boots stood in rows
held in shape with blocks of wood. Beneath was a

long drawer, locked. She wondered if it was the wardrobe he had sat in with Gus. There was a smell of cigars and cinnamon trapped within its dark recesses. She reached with inquisitive fingers into the pocket of the blue overcoat and withdrew them, running upstairs disgusted at her curiosity.

William spun fantasies about the child they were going to have. It was bound to be a girl. They would call it Catherine. When Ann grew bigger, he would massage her stomach with olive oil to stop her skin from stretching. "Baby-maker" he called her, turning her this way and that in the bed, and sometimes hurting her.

She received a second letter from Gerald. The friends with the cabin in the mountains knew of an apartment outside the campus. It was only two rooms but it would do to start with.

"What's it mean?" she asked William. "Why doesn't he mention my letter?"

"He can't face up to it," William said. "There's some people made like that." He put the letter into a drawer of his desk and told her to forget about it.

She could tell now when William wanted to see Edna. He became restless and unable to concentrate on the television. "Have you got to go out?" Ann would say, wanting to help him. "You can, you know. I don't mind." He would hug her, rub his hands over her still flat stomach and tell her she was a great girl, his girl. She was lonely without him. Having left her job at the BBC, she saw no one but him. She had tried to keep in touch with Olive, but she couldn't go out to meet her for fear of missing time with William, and she didn't want to ask Olive to the flat; Olive was round and busty, and men liked her on sight.

Mrs. Kershaw came up twice, but only to see William—once about a valve in her tyre and another time about something personal. She didn't say what it was.

"How's the pottery?" asked Ann.

"Bloody awful," said Mrs. Kershaw. A week later Pamela telephoned to say she had rented a room overlooking Regents Park. She hadn't found it comfortable in Clapham. George had been elusive.

"Pamela," said Ann. "I've missed a period. What should I feel?"

"What do you mean?"

"Well, what symptoms should I have?"

"Have your breasts gone hard?" said Pamela after a pause.

"Not really," said Ann. Pamela knew she hadn't any breasts worth speaking of.

"Do you feel sick?"

"No."

"Does your tummy feel swollen?"

It was no use. Ann hadn't any swellings. Nor had she an appetite.

"Perhaps it's all right," said Pamela. "Perhaps it's imagination."

Dutifully, Ann asked her to supper. Pamela refused. Reluctantly she gave her phone number and promised she would keep in touch and pop round when she felt more sociable. She was taking stock of herself, the life she had led. "I've been a fool," she said.

"I wouldn't say that," Ann said seriously. "There

are always people who live differently from others
—who live more dangerously. Somebody has to
lead."

There was a slight pause.

After a moment Pamela said, "That's rubbish.
Everybody's doing the same thing. You're not leading anybody. You're following."

It wasn't what Ann wanted to hear. If she was
having an illegitimate child, she needed to be
unique; she couldn't possibly be following a trend.

Pamela said she was about to take a job as a dental
receptionist. A friend of a friend knew someone
who needed one.

"That's useful," said Ann. "If I am pregnant, I'll
come to you." She knew the importance of caring
for the teeth when bearing a child. "Mummy lost all
hers when she had me," she told Pamela.

"All of them. Why?"

"Septicaemia of the blood. She had every one
extracted two weeks before I was born."

"No wonder she doesn't like you," said Pamela.

*

William's play was to tour the provinces in January
—Liverpool, Newcastle, Glasgow. He would accom-
pany the cast some of the time. Bearing in mind that
he had said they must never be parted, even for a
day, Ann looked forward to the travelling. She had
never been up north.

"Will your parents like me?" she asked. She had
a picture in her head of Mr. McClusky in his General's uniform, outside the tenements, his trumpet to

his lips. "Will they understand about Edna?"

"They've never met Edna," he admitted. "I never got round to telling them I'd split up with Sheila. But I'll take you to a football match. I'll take you to Hampden Park—after Christmas, my beauty."

It was something she had been trying to push out of her mind. She knew she would have to go home to Brighton; she had always gone home for Christmas. Mrs. Walton would never put up with her refusing to come. She might even arrive at the flat to bear her away forcibly. Hesitantly she told William that she couldn't get out of it.

"You know I don't want to go," she said. "Not with our baby coming. But I don't see what excuse I can make." She longed to say that if only William would discuss, let alone consider, divorce, things would be easier, less complicated, but she hadn't the courage. "My Mother's super," she said. "She's a wonderful person, really. But she's had a disappointing life . . . I don't want to upset her."

Till she put it into words she hadn't known how disappointed Mrs. Walton had been. With her gaiety, her passion for card games, it was she who should have met someone like William, years ago when she was young; she would never have run home for Christmas.

"You could tell her you've met someone you'd rather be with," said William. He didn't look at her.

"Oh no," she said instantly. "I can't. I can't do that."

"It's maybe for the best," he said slowly. "There's my bairns. I ought to spend time with them. And Edna's son will be coming with his wife."

He was out a lot, seeing to changes in the script, looking at costume designs, approving the sets. The phone never stopped ringing. They were usually women who called. Sometimes they asked was she Edna; once, was she Sheila. William said the whole of the English theatre world was staffed by women and they were all bloody fools. She was not to take any notice; he knew who she was and that was all that mattered. He was angling for the out-of-work Gus to play a small part in one of the pool-room scenes—amongst the old men bothered by the dust on the table—but there was a difficulty about Equity membership. A friend of William's from Glasgow days had been engaged as touring manager; someone he had known four years ago was doing the lighting. He seemed to have a lot of friends. When people telephoned they asked for Sweet William.

"Try to understand," he said. "I know it's not easy for you. But I've worked hard for this, I really have. It doesn't look much, I grant you"—he touched the few stacked sheets on his desk bearing the title of his play—"but it represents a lot of work. I did it on my own, in the wee hours, not knowing if anyone would bother to read it."

She wanted to say he hadn't been alone, that Edna had been there cooking him meals. Or Sheila, or the woman who had knitted the scarf in bands of blue.

He gave her a fur coat, not the beaver lamb, but one made out of pony skin, in brown and white. It might have been rabbit; the white parts were yellowish and it didn't suit her complexion. She wore it when she went in a taxi to the bank with him. He had

on his blue overcoat, and when he got out of the taxi
he was covered in strands of saffron-coloured fur.
She had moulted all over him. He said it didn't
matter, but she felt it was her fault. She watched him
go through the doors, picking fastidiously at the
fluff on his expensive lapels. He slapped his shoulders vigorously and pieces of fur floated upwards
and caught on his lip.

He brought home a pair of chinese slippers for
her. They reminded her of Edna's, except these
were made of red satin. She liked them, but she
wore them as little as possible.

As an early Christmas present he gave her a vari-
ety of geranium in a pot. It was five foot high. He
said it was a symbol of their love, and she watched
it on the window sill, leaves reaching towards the
light, terrified it might wilt and die. Every day she
watered it. Dennis Law on the wall behind, framed
in gilt, stood with his arms crossed on his football
shirt, fragmented by foliage and the pale sea-green
stems.

She looked up the word "conception" in one of
William's medical dictionaries on the shelf. It was
an old book and there was a drawing of something
that looked like a bunch of grapes. It said one of the
first signs of approaching motherhood was a decided languor.

"I haven't got that, have I?" she said.

"You're bone idle," said William. "You and Gus
are the idlest people I know."

She was hurt, though she tried to hide it. She
hadn't thought she was lazy.

Occasionally, the book said, there could be a

good deal of spitting of a frothy, cottonlike substance. Nothing so sensational happened to her. However, she began, every morning around six o'clock, to retch into the lavatory.

"You won't love me anymore," she gasped, nauseous above the procelain bowl. But William wiped her mouth with his hand and laid her down on the bed and told her she was his Michaelmas daisy girl.

One morning there was a letter in the hall addressed to her. She didn't know the writing. William was still asleep. He had been away for the night, staying with his producer in Windsor. He had meant to come home, but the producer's car had broken down on the way to the station and they'd missed the last train. He hadn't gone back to the house; he had stayed all night in the waiting room and had breakfast in the railway cafeteria and caught the seven o'clock to London. There was a beautiful graveyard near the producer's house, but he hadn't gone to look at it. He knew she would want him to come home. Quite important people ate in the cafeteria, even at that hour in the morning: poets and solicitors—a biographer he knew with blue eyes. Everywhere William went he met someone he knew.

She opened the letter in the sitting room. It said—

My Dear Ann,
You are younger than I. Time stretches ahead of you. Don't take my husband. I need him. I have no life waiting for me in America. I beg you, give him back to me. I feel as if I am locked away in prison. The nights are so long, the sentence so savage. I

112

don't know what I am being punished for. I dream of being free but someone must be waiting for me when I come out.

Forgive me,
Edna.

Ann read it again. Tears filled her eyes and splashed onto the notepaper. The ink ran. She went into the bedroom and shook William by the shoulder. His skin was honey-coloured, his eyes startled.

"Jesus," he said. "Let me be."

She tugged at the bedding. She told him to get up.

"What's wrong," he asked, stumbling naked into the sitting room and collapsing onto the sofa. He sat with the letter on his knees. There was a blue vein in his leg, a tuft of ginger hair beneath the pout of his belly.

He spent a long time explaining that Edna had no justification for writing in that way. It was emotional blackmail of the worst sort. Ann was to put it from her mind. Edna had married him, been loved, was still cared for. If he had chosen to fall in love with someone else, she couldn't hope to hold him by force. He thrust his arm, in a gesture of liberation, outwards, with fish clenched. He looked military and unloving. She didn't care for his use of the word "chosen," as if he had picked her deliberately from the group of women in the church hall, instead of dropping willy nilly, besotted by feelings, into her life.

"But she sounds so unhappy," she cried, looking down at the sad letter on his knee.

113

"Don't be taken in," he said fiercely. "Look at the calculated splodge on that particular sentence." He read aloud—"Someone must be waiting for me." He flung the letter contemptuously to the floor and said she had probably held the paper under the tap to make it seem tear-stained. Ann wanted to correct him, but he sounded so vindictive, as if for the first time his love for Edna was wavering. She didn't want to prevent that.

"Maybe," she said, drying her eyes on the back of her hand. "All the same, I do feel . . . shabby."

Secretly she would have liked to reply to Edna, saying she was having a baby but she would go away at once. She was unable to, because she feared Edna would show her letter to William and because, being pregnant, there was nowhere to go. She toyed with the idea of buying a ticket to America, jumping into bed with Gerald, having a premature child. But it would be blond and snub-nosed, and the energy required for such an undertaking was beyond her. Maybe she was bone idle, as William had suggested. William promised he would not be too hard on Edna, but he would point out how foolish she had been to send such an emotional plea for security. "After all," he said. "I'm not a dummy for her mouth. I'm not a comforter."

His reaction, Ann supposed, was splendid. Still, he didn't explain why he hadn't told Edna she was having a child. Considering he ate there three times a week, she would have thought he might have mentioned it.

He stumped back to bed, weary after his night in Windsor, and slept till the afternoon.

114

*

As the preparations for the provincial tour progressed, William became morose. He picked at his food. He catnapped on the sofa. He stopped buying new clothes; he took to wearing the torn sweaters he had owned when Ann met him, the plimsolls without laces. She liked him better out of his tasteful suits, his shoes of real leather, the alien, successful overcoat. Apart from her pony skin and her blue smock, she had few clothes herself. As she didn't go out much, except to do the shopping, it hardly mattered.

He had taken her once to have breakfast in a little café, next door to the tobacco kiosk on the Finchley Road. They ordered bacon-and-egg and tomatoes. Though it was barely nine o'clock in the morning, he poured H.P. sauce onto his plate. She felt sick. He ate with his knife and fork held like two pencils; she could hardly bear to look. She hadn't noticed it at home. It was so common. "William," she said. He looked up. He was hunched low over his food, his mouth shiny with grease. "I don't like to mention it . . . please forgive me . . . but couldn't you . . ." She went red in the face. "Jesus," he said in alarm. "What's up?" When she told him, when she suggested he should tuck the handles of the cutlery into his palm, his eyes widened. "It's important is it?" he said. "Yes," she whispered. He held his elbows to his sides and pointed his fingers down the middle of the knife. "That's lovely," she said. He was very quiet, very subdued. Now and then she caught him looking at her with a curiously sad expression in his

115

pale eyes. He's embarrassed, she thought, that he's let me down.

Before he grew depressed he had intended to take her to rehearsals, to have dinner with the cast. But he was too upset about his play.

"It's not good enough," he said, striding up and down the sitting room, his hands clasped behind his back. "When they first read it, it was pretty powerful —know what I mean? It had something. Now I'm not so sure."

His hair had grown again. It curled on his neck, wound in tendrils about his small ears.

"It's just you've heard it too often," said Ann. She hadn't read the play all through—she pretended she had—only that one scene in the billiard hall.

He said, "I can't pinpoint what's wrong. But it's false. The girl who plays Moira is no good. She's got a plum in her mouth. She was never born in a tenement."

Ann was glad he was displeased with Moira. She had visualised her as perfect and talented. She kept thinking of him at rehearsals, chatting to the cast, the men and the women, complimenting them on their hair, tugging at their clothing and asking was it Donegal tweed. She saw quite clearly Pamela on the sofa, convalescing, and William taking the turkish necklace between his fingers, twisting it toward the light, the edge of his hand brushing the soft skin of her throat.

"Some of it's all right," he said. "But pieces of it are just no good."

"What pieces?" she asked, trying to be helpful.

He took the script from the desk. He shuffled the

pages until he found the dialogue that disappointed him. He had no need to read it—he knew it by heart:

"You're restless, Gus."
"Aye, I'm restless."
"What's making you restless, then?"
"I canna tell. I'm just restless."

Ann wondered why all his characters repeated themselves so often. And why was the man called Gus? Why not Jock or Hamish?

"You're going away fra' me."
"I'm not going away fra' you, woman."
"Aye, you're going away. I know it here."

"That's very nice," said Ann.
"Wait," he said impatiently. "Wait."
He stood with hunched shoulders and lips aggressive.

"I feel as if you're going away, and I'm locked up. Walled up, maybe. When I come out, I'm wondering will there be anyone waiting?"

It was real, Ann thought. It was reminiscent of something. She didn't know what, but it struck a chord. She did feel for Moira.
"I don't see why you're critical," she said truthfully. "I think it's wonderful. I do really."
But he wasn't convinced. He stuck the script under some newspapers and stared out of the window. She would have liked to help him, but she wasn't

equipped. He was so good to her, so loving. He made her swallow her vitamins; he encouraged her to drink glasses of orange juice. She was only seven weeks pregnant, but he suggested she learn to knit.

"I can't," she said bashfully. "I can't knit."

So he bought some needles and a ball of pink wool and began to fashion a small drooping garment, vest or dress, that might have fitted a doll.

He telephoned her two evenings later from a call box. He sounded agitated. "I'm on the Watford bypass."

"What are you doing there?"

"I'm not sure. I'm just here. I just had to get away."

"Don't leave me," she cried out, careless of Roddy in the downstairs flat. Her eyes stung with tears of self-pity.

"I'm not going away from you. I'm getting away from my play. Don't you see that?"

She couldn't answer.

"Ann . . . Ann . . . Don't let me down."

"I'm sorry," she said. "Have you got your scarf with you?"

It didn't matter who had knitted it for him, just as long as he was protected against the December wind.

"I have," he said. "That's one thing I have."

He was trying to tell her something. She mustn't let him down. "Little boy," she said. "Don't worry . . . I'm here."

"Dear Jesus," he said, and hung up.

She telephoned Pamela almost at once. Her fingers as she dialed were numb with cold. Beyond the porch the privet hedge heaved in the wind. William was marching, with pallid lips, towards Watford.

Pamela sounded as if she had been woken from a dream; she didn't seem to be able to speak properly. Yet she couldn't have been in bed: the radio was on; there was music in the background.

"Who is it?"

"It's me—Ann."

She could hear Pamela breathing, the mournful strains of a violin.

"I can't take it. I don't really understand him. He's gone walking."

Silence.

"Pamela . . . are you there. Pamela?"

After a moment Pamela said distantly—"Yes."

"Where do you think he's gone? Where's he gone?"

"Perhaps he's looking at graveyards," said Pamela. "He likes graveyards, doesn't he?"

Ann had forgotten about graveyards. "But it's dark," she said.

There was another long moment of silence. *Tum te tum tum tum te tum* went the piano in the background. "Say something," she begged. "Please say something."

"I can't," said Pamela. The receiver was replaced.

4

Ann went home to Brighton, unwillingly, two days
before Christmas. William promised to water the
geranium when she was gone. He bought presents
for her parents—a book on military campaigns,
bound in leather, a fur stole for her mother. She
couldn't be sure how Mrs. Walton would react. She
might insist on it being returned.

"It's lovely," Ann said, aghast at his generosity.
"It's just the sort of thing she likes."

She wouldn't allow William to wait on the platform until the train departed; she kissed him at the
window and urged him not to forget to take the
sheets to the laundry. He was wearing a new tweed
jacket and a cap to match, with a little jaunty brim.
He looked broad shouldered and sporty; he had a
woollen tie, leather gloves buttoned at the wrist.
She herself, by comparison, was careless and un-
stitched; her skirt hung below the hem of the new
coat; the boots that William had bought her, of

black leather, lined with crimson, gaped on her thin legs. She was eclipsed. She felt like some strange hybrid insect, with her sticklike limbs, her fur body moulting at the window, drifting above the grey platform. Relieved, she watched him stride away, turn under the clock, wave his last fond farewell. On the kitchen table she had left him a surprise, a present wrapped in green shiny paper, tied with ribbon. It was an electric shaver. There was a letter with it, saying she knew things had been difficult lately— her disturbing dreams, his play, her possessiveness —but she loved him very much.

Her father met her at the station. He laid his cold lips against her cold cheek. He put her suitcases in the boot of the small car and drove her home to Mummy.

The house was in a terrace, three streets away from the sea front. It was made of brick with a front door painted yellow. In the summer months Mrs. Walton put up a gay shade of canvas to protect the paintwork from the sunshine and the salt air. There was a Christmas tree in the bay window, threaded with lights and coloured balls.

"Darling," cried Mrs. Walton, throwing open the door and laughing immoderately. In her cocktail dress of green rayon, her earrings, she was every inch the hostess. Across her nose was an orange smear of powder, near-sightedly applied.

The banisters shone, the tufted rugs half-mooned the hearths set with electric fires. All doors were open, to the sitting room, the dining room, the kitchen: glimpses of tables and chairs, chintz cushions, bowls of fruit. Everything burnished and glowing—mahogany sideboard, the bronze statue of the angels wrestling, the apples and the tangerines piled on the baskets made of silver plate. Above the wall-to-wall carpeting, flecked with purple, the looped streamers quivered in the heat. What trouble her mother had gone to, to make it seem like home. The fur was admired, the boots. "My word," said her mother. "We have been throwing our money about." Reluctantly Ann removed her coat. The thistledown flew about the hall. She held her breath and clasped her hands on her stomach.

"You've lost weight," her mother said. "You've been working too hard."

Supper time was festive, with a glass of sherry to celebrate her homecoming, and ham cut from the bone. George Patterson had been in hospital with heart trouble. Aimée Hughes had had a breast removed. Mrs. Munro's sister's child had produced a baby without arms. Mrs. Glendenning had gone peacefully in her sleep—the only way to go. Mrs. Munro herself was being treated for hypertension.

"Why?" asked Ann, shocked.

"Nerves. She runs the whist-drives. She does all her own gardening."

"The baby—" said Ann, but Mrs. Walton grimaced in the direction of her husband, as if the subject was too delicate.

She had tickets for the church pantomime. The Floral Hall was cold, and Captain Walton kept on his muffler and his overcoat with the band of velvet at the collar. Everyone chatted to Mrs. Walton—the vicar's wife, Aimée Hughes, wearing an apron crisscrossed upon her mutilated chest, Mrs. Munro. She was so popular, so well known. She ran gaily between the rows of chairs to the trestle table set with cups and sandwiches. She laid her hand on the vicar's arm as he passed. She admonished the choirboys slithering excitedly over the worn planking of the wooden floor.

"You've met my daughter, haven't you?" she cried, above the noise of the cups placed on saucers, the chairs dragged into place. "Works in London, you know. For the BBC."

Ann smiled and bobbed and shook hands. Her mother's laugh, high-pitched and near hysteria, leapt and trembled about the hall. Captain Walton, ignored, tapped his feet for warmth; his eyelids flickered, his lips turned blue. The curtains opened and the local ballet school, in green and white, danced with precision. The leading lady, dressed as Robinson Crusoe, cast herself beneath a papier-mâché tree and sang "One Day My Ship Will Come." The church organist, Arnold Mason, played "Man Friday." He rolled his eyes comically and bounded like a dog about the stage. Whenever he opened his mouth to speak, Mrs. Walton gasped in anticipation and dug Ann in the ribs. She led the laughter and the applause.

In the interval everyone agreed that Arnold Mason was a scream. Ann would have liked to be friendly, to have joined in. When her parents had settled in Brighton she had been away at school—she had no roots, no continuity; she knew none of the young couples arm in arm in the back rows, united by churchgoing and tennis tournaments. She smiled till her jaws ached. Now she was here, with her mother the life and soul of the party, she wondered why she had come—why she had left William in London to spend Christmas alone. Perhaps it was her father she had made the journey for. She put her arm through his in the darkness. He shifted on his chair. After a few moments he had a fit of coughing and removed his arm to get at his handkerchief. When he had recovered he crossed his arms on his chest.

Later, Mrs. Walton sat Ann in the kitchen and said, "Now, tell me about him—this person you were so full of."

It was an apt phrase. Bent over her stomach, Ann tried not to feel hostile. Her mother had the knack of stemming communication at source. Like frost, she nipped the bud before it had time to open.

"He's just a writer."

"Have you met the father yet?"

"Not yet. But next month he's taking me to meet him."

Her mother didn't mention Mr. McClusky's rank. Maybe she feared he wasn't a General after all, and it was best to live under an illusion. She was no fool. "How rich is he?"

"Quite rich. He bought that coat . . . and the boots. He's got you a lovely present for Christmas."

"Me? Me?" Amazed, Mrs. Walton pushed her hand against her breast. She clutched her sapphire brooch.

"And something for Father. He's very generous."

"Show me the present. Let me see it." The little spiky lashes, blobbed with mascara, blinked rapidly above greedy eyes.

125

"You'll have to wait," said Ann.

"I want to see it now."

"You can't, Mummy."

The electric fires were switched off, the lights on the Christmas tree extinguished; the warmth faded from the terrace house. The mist rolled in from the sea front, penetrating the doors and the windows.

"I'm cold," Ann complained, climbing the stairs.

"Rubbish," said her mother. "It's very mild."

She flung open the window of the bedroom, adjusted the rug beside the divan, turned back the sheet.

"Can't I close the window?" Ann said.

"No, leave it open. It's stuffy in here."

Captain Walton coughed in the back bedroom.

"Sssh," said her mother. "Don't disturb your father. Get into bed quick and turn the light off. Don't leave your clothes all over the floor."

Ann looked at her room, at the neat net curtains, the picture on the wall, taken from a calendar, of two kittens on a cushion. On the dressing table was a sewing basket she had used at school. That was all, apart from the bed and a chair. No books, no dolls, no hockey stick or tennis racket. All her childhood tidied away.

She could hear her mother opening the door of the walnut wardrobe, the metallic noise as she replaced her brooch among the other jewelry, the rustle of polythene as she hung her dress safely against moth, the click of the switch as she turned off her electric blanket, a faint vulgar noise of wind escaping.

126

*

Mrs. Walton opened William's present before anyone else's. She fingered the fur, looked for a label. Ann watched her face.

"It's very nice," she said finally, and laid it to one side. She wasn't going to return it, but obviously it was not as expensive as Ann had imagined.

At the bottom of her suitcase Ann had discovered a small box with her name written on the lid. Inside was a string of amber beads and a square of white card—"To my own darling from your loving William." Ann left the beads and the note where her mother might see them. When she looked an hour later, the necklace had been placed on the mantelpiece. Beside it lay the remains of the card, torn into pieces.

Aunt Bea and Uncle Walter came for Christmas lunch. They sat in the front room with crackers beside each plate and the meat on the sideboard. There was very little space. The cord for the electric carving knife stretched like a trip wire across the hearth. The chairs backed on to the electric fire; Mrs. Walton was forever leaning sideways, fondling the polished legs, to see if the wood was scorched. Captain Walton carved standing up and stopped frequently to cough. Whenever he did, Mrs. Walton jumped up and rubbed the misted surface of the sideboard with her napkin. Ann wore rouge on her cheeks. She had woken at dawn in a room filled with fog and retched into her handkerchief. Her lips tasted of salt.

"Pamela's in London, then?" said Mrs. Walton, not too sharply.

"Working," said Aunt Bea, defensively. "She's a dental receptionist now. In Regents Park."

"Surely not on Christmas Day?"

"She has a lot of friends," said Aunt Bea. She looked sideways at Ann, as if to imply it was different for her.

"No stuffing," said Uncle Walter. "If that's no trouble."

"And how's your young man?" asked Aunt Bea. "The professor."

"He's well," Ann said. "He's made friends with some people who have a cabin in the mountains. They shoot bears."

"It's illegal," remarked Walter. "It's not on."

"They do shoot," said Ann. "I may have got the animal wrong."

"Have you ever met Richard Murdoch?" he said. "In the course of your work."

"No," said Ann. He asked the same question every Christmas: he had been in the RAF during the war, and had once seen Richard Murdoch across the room at a tea-dance.

Mrs. Walton swept up crumbs from the carpet and emptied the ashtrays, even while they were eating. She crawled on hands and knees under the table with her pan and brush.

Aunt Bea admired the clay bowl on the windowsill that Ann had given her mother.

"There's a lady in the downstairs flat from Ann," explained Mrs. Walton, "who's a potter. She's very artistic."

"It's strange how so many of them are," said Aunt Bea. "In London. Pamela's been living until recently with a lady in Hampstead who does modern dance."

"In Hampstead?" said Ann.

"What the hell is modern dance?" asked Walter, coarse with drink.

"She's a frightfully nice woman. Very well spoken. I've talked to her on the phone once or twice."

"I didn't know," Ann said. "I thought Pamela was in Regents Park."

Walter jumped up and sang a chorus from "Much Binding in the Marsh." He tripped over the wrought-iron magazine stand and sent it backwards into the alcove. Aunt Bea pushed him into an armchair and he fell asleep with his mouth open. His hands trembled on his lap.

Mrs. Walton lit a cigarette and squinted upwards through the smoke. Ash fell onto her breast. She looked down at the opening of her dress and stroked her skin lovingly with the tips of her scarlet fingernails.

If only I was adopted, thought Ann. If only they could tell me now, this moment, like an extra gift, that I was not flesh of their flesh, but different. How peaceful that would be. She was so like them. She possessed in equal quantities, the reticence of her father, the vampire instincts of her mother. Already her face, shaped like her father's, was stamped with the character of her mother. She had only to lift an eyebrow, shrug her shoulders. I'm having a baby, she thought, choking on a silver sixpence sticky in a wedge of Christmas pudding. A bastard.

They listened to the Queen's speech. Her father didn't stand to attention; he sat up stiffly in his chair, eyes front, gazing stoically at the net curtains and the grey sky beyond.

Later they drove along the coast to a beauty resort—in summer: now the wind tore across the flattened grass and rocked the car where it stood. They walked to the headland. Aunt Bea and Mrs. Walton turned back almost at once. They struggled, the ends of their headscarves whipping their outraged faces, back to the car and Walter, snoring, with his head against the window. Above the beach was a fragile structure of wood, cut into steps, leading down to the shore. It creaked, shifted, whined under the thunderous onslaught of the wind. The sea smashed against the cliffs, leapt into the air, fell away, leaving a strip of umber sand, laced with foam. Captain Walton began to descend the steps. He clung to the driftwood rail with both hands, his muffler streaming behind him. "Don't," shouted Ann. He screamed something in reply—she couldn't hear: it was typical of him to become articulate when atmospheric conditions rendered her deaf. She followed him. Maybe, she thought, her father would like William: they both knew so much about Napoleon, the desert, the vulnerability of men under fire. He had unwrapped the book on military campaigns, fondled the leather, looked up with baffled eyes. He had never asked who had given it to him, never read the inscription on the inside page.

She cowered under the spray that rose into the

air, gasping for breath. They stumbled down the last wooden flight, jumped onto the beach and turned their backs on the incoming sea. Their clothes were saturated. She got earache almost at once. She stamped upon the sand and clutched her head. The cliff rose in tiers and shelved the sea to the north. When the tide was out and the day was calm, people lay in bathing costumes under the sun. Children ran like cats upon damp ground, skipping fastidiously on frail and tender feet over the baked ridges of the beach. "Stand fast," cried Captain Walton, and they leaned against the white cliff and the sea rolled up and hit them in the back. He held his arms up over his head in a gesture of surrender. She nearly fell, sucked backwards by the water. She ballooned outwards, the baby growing inside her, the heart pumping blood. The sea dropped away. They were still alive, wet through and trembling. He led her to the steps, tiptoeing through the receding waves, his hand urgent on her elbow. They dragged themselves upwards. How dangerous it had been. She wondered what had possessed him to go down onto the shore. They could have been drowned.

Mrs. Walton was almost speechless with irritation. They made so much mess inside the car; they dripped onto the upholstery. Ann's fur was ruined. Ruined. "You careless girl," she cried, touching over and over the matted shoulders, the doused collar. A chemical smell, like bleach, filled the travelling car. Such trouble they had caused—the expense of the water heater for baths, the drying of clothes.

In the dismal garden she pegged Captain Walton's overcoat onto the line; it swung, stiff with salt, to and fro above the waterlogged grass.

On Boxing Day, after lunch, Mrs. Walton became aggressive. It was a strain having a grown child in the house.

"Have you written to that person in America?" she asked. "About this new male . . . this writer." She sounded as if she would be angry at a negative reply.

"Yes," said Ann. "I've told him I can't go."

"You foolish girl," scolded her mother. "You could have waited till you had seen which way the land lay."

"I couldn't," Ann said. "William wouldn't let me. He told me to write."

"My husband," began Mrs. Walton, "during the war—"

"My father," said Ann.

"—tried to make me write to my friend the rear-gunner. I wouldn't."

"But in the end—" said Ann.

"It was utterly different. It was the war. I told my father about it—"

"My grandfather," Ann said. It was not so much that she was trying to define relationships as that she wanted her mother to be less possessive. She needed to be included.

"—he said it was none of his business."

Was it always like that, Ann wondered. Did people endlessly choose the same kind of people to love? Her grandfather, it seemed, had, like her own father, avoided involvement. Once the big Victorian family had been swept away—the wide scope of aunts and uncles and cousins—did the choice narrow? Did you trudge around in an inner-circle waiting for the one person who reminded you of your father? Did William think, deep inside, that she was none of his business?

"Have you given yourself to him?" asked Mrs. Walton.

"Only once," said Ann. It sounded better, limiting the number of times.

"You disgust me," said her mother. She turned off the electric fire.

"Don't," protested Ann. "I'm cold."

"Nonsense."

"I am. You never stop to think about anyone else. You're so selfish." She was shouting.

"Behave yourself," said her mother firmly. "Just because you're living a very undisciplined life and being made unhappy in consequence, you have no cause to turn on me. I've told you before. You're your own worst enemy." The corkscrew curls sprang backwards from the complacent face. The plump hands, circled with diamond ring and platinum watch, beat a tattoo on her crossed knee.

"I'm freezing," whimpered Ann. They struggled with the switch on the fire, clicked it on and off, childishly. Her mother won.

"Why did you tear up my card?" Ann cried. "You had no right."

"What card?"

"My card." Tears ran down her cheeks.

"My dear girl," said her mother. "You need something for your nerves. You're imagining things. There's something radically wrong with you." And she peered with genuine concern at the miserable face, blotched with weeping.

"William," said Ann, "says you've tried to devour me."

There was a pause. Her mother stared at the floor. "If he knows you so well," she said, "why hasn't he mentioned wedding bells?"

"He's married," said Ann.

In the front room, napping in the chair, Captain Walton coughed.

"Why does he cough so much?" she asked.

"To gain attention," said Mrs. Walton. "To gain attention." She stretched her legs across the rug. The fire had mottled them, patterned the shins with purple.

"William loves me," said Ann. "He really does."

"You need more than love, my girl. When you were born, I lost all my teeth."

"I know," Ann said, remorseful. "But William loves me."

"Love," said Mrs. Walton scornfully.

"He's going to ask his wife for a divorce."

"When?"

"Soon."

"Rubbish."

"I don't understand you," said Ann. "Don't you want me to be happy?"

"Go to hell," said Mrs. Walton.

*

She couldn't ring William to say she was returning a day earlier, because she didn't want to be overheard and detained. When her mother had gone four doors away to visit Aimée Hughes, Ann told her father she was leaving.

"Oh," he said. "Something cropped up?"

"Sort of," she said.

She ran to the station and waited three hours for a train. She watched the end of the platform for her father to appear, sent by her mother. He never came. By the time she was seated in the train she remembered only the warmth of the house when she had arrived, the little gifts in her stocking at the end of the bed, the orange in tissue paper, the chocolate mouse.

*

She took a taxi to Nethersole Road. The house was in darkness save for a light in the hall. Mrs. Kershaw's bicycle lay against the wardrobe; there was mud on the wheels, a new lamp on the handlebars. She fitted her key into the lock, stepped from the green carpeting of the landing onto the black and white tiles. The bedroom door was open; there was a body, two bodies, lying on the bed. She stopped, the suitcase still in her hand. She walked into the far corner of the sitting room to turn on the light. There was a faint click in the hall as if someone had gone out, a rustle from the bedroom. The geranium on the window ledge was dying: the stems hung down; through the pale and wrinkled leaves stared

Dennis Law. The doorbell rang. It was William.

"You," he said. "Why didn't you let me know?" He put his arms round her; he pressed her head against his shoulder.

"There's someone in the bedroom," she whispered. "A man and a woman. I thought it was you."

He looked startled. He sat her on the sofa and went into the bedroom. She heard him say—"Oh it's you, Mrs. Kershaw. Is there anything wrong?" And Mrs. Kershaw replied, "There's a leak. In the roof. Roddy asked me to see what damage there was."

She came into the sitting room in the familiar dressing gown tied with string, her short hair untidy. There was a smear of clay on her sandal. The conversation was about Christmas, about presents. Ann looked at the pattern of the carpet. Three borders, a space—her mother loved the earthenware bowl—another two borders, another space—her mother had been speechless over the fur stole—three large squares, each with a border repeated in alternate bands of reddish brown and blue: how intricate it was. Her father had read the book on military campaigns from cover to cover. Her skirt, hanging in folds above the calves of her black boots, cast a large purple shadow. In the shadow she saw two shapes, or was it one? William and Pamela. Now, why Pamela? William had just this moment come home and Mrs. Kershaw had been examining the ceiling for damp. In the dark.

"I don't like this place anymore," she said out loud.

William unbuttoned her coat, unzipped her boots. They were no longer black and supple; the sea had bleached them. Maybe they weren't real leather. He went on talking about Christmas, the walks he had taken with his children on the Heath, flying a kite, pushing a dog on wheels. During this, Mrs. Kershaw went downstairs—one moment she was there and the next moment the chair was empty, if she had ever been there at all. Ann watched William stroke the surface of her ruined coat.

"It fell in the sea," she said.

"No matter," said William. "We can have it restored."

"I thought it was Pamela," she said.

He touched her face. "What's wrong girl?" he asked. "You're so nervy. It's not like you to imagine things. What ails you?"

She frowned deeply.

"Is it the baby?"

She shook her head and gave a fleeting smile to indicate the baby was lovely and dear to her heart. She grew sullen again; her mouth dropped. After a moment she said, "I'm not a fool, you know."

"No," he agreed. "You're not a fool."

She opened her mouth to say she had seen him on the bed. His thumb clung to her lip. "My mother was dreadful to me. And my father. They know something's up." She stared at him accusingly.

"You told them about the baby?"

"What do you mean?" She was indignant at his stupidity. "How could I? My mother's furious with me. I told her you were married and that was bad enough. She turned all the fires off in the house. I was freezing."

He said, "But it's warm now."

"She said why didn't you mention wedding bells."

"Ah," he said.

He stopped touching her face and squatted on his heels, rocking backwards and forwards with his hands brushing the carpet. But he said nothing else. There were no sounds in the whole house, no aeroplanes in the sky, no dogs barking on the squares of grass. The lack of talk, of words, was like a great chasm appearing in the floor. There was nothing but darkness.

"Did you have nice walks with the children?" she asked. Anything to step backwards from the chasm.

"Ann," he said. "I'm sorry your mother was upset about me being a married man. If she hurt you on my account, then I'm ashamed. I've failed you." He was dreadfully serious, mature; she was moved by him. She wasn't going to forgive him immediately, but she did feel happier.

"But," he persisted, lip thrust out, brow furrowed, "if you're sore on your own account, I can't help you." His mouth snapped shut, like a trap.

She looked down at him, baffled.

"It's not your mother's business if you're having a love affair with a married man," he continued. "She can feel concern for you, I grant you. But it's nothing to do with her. You're a grown woman. Having a baby is nothing to do with your mother, either. Not your kind of mother, leastways."

138

She went cold inside at the implication that she had made her mother out to be a monster. It was as if she was in the next room, listening to every word.

"But it is," she protested. "The shame—"

"It's her shame," he said quietly, moderately. "Not yours."

It was like one of his plays.

There was a knot tied in the cord of the electric light that she hadn't noticed before. The brown leaves of the dead geranium lay sprawled upon the windowsill. He'd taken out the bulb from the centre lamp because he said the light was too harsh.

"I don't mean shame," she muttered.

"Aye," he said. "You do mean shame." Any moment now he would start talking about dust. "I don't blame you. You've led a very unrealistic sort of existence. You see things differently from the rest of us."

"I know what I saw in there," she cried out, jerking her head in the direction of the bedroom. "I know that. And you not mentioning you had another wife, and people ringing up all the time and you keeping your voice low."

He jumped to his feet. He clenched his fists. "Ann, Ann," he said sorrowfully. "Believe me, it's all in your head. I'm not like that. You've made me up."

She sat there, looking at him. Her face wore a distressed uncertain smile.

"I'm not your man in America, Ann. I'm not your mother. I'm me." And he thumped his fist on the front of his washed out sweater, scowling at her.

"I'm pregnant," she said. The tears ran down her

cheeks and her mouth opened in a wail of misery.

"I didn't force you," he pointed out. "I never walked in here against your will. You met my wife, you let me through that door."

He flung his arm out, pointing it towards the hallway, meaning the door of the flat, but all she could see was the pink bedroom that he had spoilt forever.

"I don't like this place," she repeated stubbornly.

She cried for a long time. He walked about the room. He cuddled her. He forced her to the floor and made love to her. The tears never stopped. He picked her up and attempted to carry her into the bedroom and she struggled and fell on the floor, scrambling back towards the sofa, as if there were wild beasts out there, in the pink and onetime lovely room. She felt better, moaning and carrying on. Sometimes she had to think of something really dreadful, like her mother being mangled under a bus, to keep the tears flowing. She was so tired. She curled up on the sofa and he crouched on the floor, holding her hand, saying it was all in her head, the bad things weren't real, everything was beautiful.

"I know," she moaned, almost asleep. She dozed. She saw Pamela standing on the gangplank of a ship, waving. "Pamela's been living in Hampstead," she said loudly, opening her eyes and tugging at his hair. "With a woman who does modern dance."

"What are you on about?" he asked, fuddled with sleep.

"That time she came," she said, "when she had a birthday. Hopping all over this room in those silly ballet slippers."

She fell asleep and when she woke in the night,

140

he was in the kitchen, his head against a green parcel tied with ribbon, his cheek stuck to the painted surface of the table.

"I want to leave here," she said. "I hate this place."

He was firm then. He laid her down on the divan and stroked her forehead. He sang "The Green Oak Tree," softly, over and over.

*

He thought she meant it. He looked for another flat.

In the daytime, when he was out, she lay down in the double bed and rested. When she heard his footstep on the stair, she leapt up and busied herself in the kitchen. The electric shaver, still in its green paper, stayed like a cruet set or vase of flowers, in the centre of the table. She reproached him about the geranium.

"You let it die," she said bitterly. "You promised to water it."

"Jesus," he exclaimed, exasperated. "It's only a plant."

He found a flat in Regents Park, though they couldn't move in for another two months.

"You'll like it," he said. "It's on the ground floor and there's a patch of garden where you can put the baby in the pram."

She didn't know what to say. As her mother would have put it, she felt she had been hoisted with her own petard. She faced Mrs. Kershaw. She went downstairs and knocked at the door. "I'm leaving," she said. "We're leaving . . . soon."

"Aye," said Mrs. Kershaw. "I know. William mentioned it. There's work to be done on the roof anyway." She fiddled with the drawstring of her gypsy blouse. "I'll have to take the ceiling down."

Ann looked at the clay pots, the dead tree against the wall. Someone had painted the word PEACE on the back of the door. She met Mrs. Kershaw's eyes. Mrs. Kershaw looked away. She said, "Perhaps, Ann, dear, it's for the best. Roddy is a little put out by William. I expect William told you."

"No," said Ann. "Is it the bicycle?"

"Roddy and William had a skirmish. He was going to the *Northern Star* on Christmas Eve, with Eric."

"I don't know Eric," said Ann.

"Roddy's friend. He's very young and emotional. William never asked Roddy if he minded."

Ann was smiling. It was wonderful to think of William on Christmas Eve, going out with someone called Eric. He could have been with Edna or Sheila or Moira—there were so many women in the world —but he'd gone with Eric.

"He came down in a tweed jacket."

"It's new," said Ann. "He has a cap to match."

"We didn't see the cap," Mrs. Kershaw said. "Only the jacket. You see, Roddy lost a parcel some time ago. A friend in Ireland sent him some tweed. Roddy chose the material himself from samples. It was woven specially. William happened to find the material on the hall table. He took it to a tailor he knew."

"Found it?" Ann said.

"That was exactly Roddy's tone of voice," said

Mrs. Kershaw. "He knocked William down."

"Hit him?" said Ann. She was horrified.

"Didn't you notice?" asked Mrs. Kershaw. "Didn't you notice his eye?"

Ann hadn't. But then William's face was never the same; it changed daily, like his clothes. "Were you really looking at the roof?" she said. If William and Roddy had come to blows, if William had stolen Roddy's length of tweed, then surely Mrs. Kershaw might be moved to tell the truth.

"I won't let the flat again, for some time," said Mrs. Kershaw. "Not until we've had the roof done."

*

Ann went back to sleeping in the bedroom. Her stomach swelled slowly. She bought a bottle of olive oil and placed it in a prominent position on the shelves above the cooker. William used it to fry his breakfast eggs. He never mentioned her stretch marks. The provincial tour had been postponed for a further six weeks. They were opening at the Palace Theatre in Newcastle. He said Ann must come to Liverpool when the cast had settled down.

"But why can't I come to Newcastle?" she asked.

"You'll be in the middle of moving. Someone has to be there when the men come to connect the gas," he said reasonably.

An American telephoned. He said his name was Chuck von Schreiber. William was out.

"I'm his wife," Ann told him. She had never said that before.

"Now look here, sweetheart," said Chuck, "tell

Willie I need to hear from him. Tell him he can contact me at Brown's Hotel."

She told William. He was excited at first. After he had spoken to the American he seemed cast down.

"He's just a bum," he said. "He's nobody special. He thinks he wants to take my play to the States."

She remembered her dreams about William leaving from airfields and docksides.

"I expect he will," she said. "Bum or no bum. If not him, then somebody else."

She wondered if she dared write to Gerald, a letter wholly from her, telling him she was engaged to be married. They had been good friends; they'd gone to the theatre together, and to a concert once at the Albert Hall. If her dreams were wrong and it was she in the shadows, waving, then she could look him up in America and they would have dinner, the three of them. She didn't write to him, however, because William had torn the address from both the letters, and she couldn't find the pieces in the drawer of his desk.

At the end of February they prepared to move into the new flat. William was more settled now that he could visualise a stage and his play upon it, with scenery and an audience and a curtain going up and down. He had arranged for a small van to collect the clothing and the books, the pictures, Mrs. Walton's pink rug. The only furniture they owned was the divan bed, the desk and the wardrobe in the hall. He said not to worry, he would buy tables and things before he left for Newcastle. She was to leave everything to him.

The weather was mild. Already there were buds

on the sycamore trees; the forsythia bush by the fence was spiked with yellow blossom. William discarded his overcoat and wore a new jacket brought up from the wardrobe in the hall, of brown and white check. It had narrow lapels and a lining of shot silk.

He was going out to the rehearsal rooms in Euston. He said he wouldn't be late, he wanted to help with the last-minute packing. The van was due at nine o'clock the next morning.

When he had gone, Ann washed the crockery that was hers and put it in a cardboard box and carried it onto the landing. She placed the clean sheets on top. She tied her books into bundles bound with string and piled them at the side of the cardboard box. Inside a suitcase, with some of her clothes, went the despised electric clock, the kettle and the electric shaver, still wrapped in Christmas paper.

She took Dennis Law and Samuel Palmer off the wall. Across the back of the footballer's frame was written in pencil—"To my own William, from Edna." She turned over Samuel Palmer but there was nothing to read. She daren't empty his desk; she longed to rifle the secretive drawer, but she hadn't the courage. It was too reminiscent of her mother.

At midday she went on to the Finchley Road and shopped. On an impulse, as she passed the hairdressers, she went in and asked if she could have a shampoo and set. She had thought they would be too busy, but they covered her shoulders with a towel and sat her at the basin; she hadn't washed her neck and she worried about it. She went scarlet under the drier. Her ears burned. An hour later she came out with lacquered waves, a small rash upon her chest. She ran with averted head and carrier bag up the hill, desperate in case she bumped into William. She doused her head under the cold water tap and dripped onto the carpet. She talked to herself as she straightened her crinkled hair. We've been married for over a year ... yes ... we met at a church hall . . . no, I haven't been here before. Oh, I love it. She smiled into the room. Oh, it means so many things, being the wife of a celebrated writer . . . travel . . . interesting friends . . . yes, I suppose my life has been enhanced. She stayed with her head on one side, the comb caught in the bedraggled strands of hair, motionless. He makes me feel alive . . . I've grown in so many ways.

She never saw Olive or Mrs. Kershaw or friends at Bush House. She hadn't any letters to read from her fiancé. She was leaving the flat she had lived in for six years. Pamela no longer came to stay. "It's as if," she said aloud, speaking now only to herself, "I'm not really here at all. I've gone funny inside somewhere. I've been taken over, requisitioned."

She walked to the window, looked down at the garden. Mrs. Kershaw was bending over the grass verge digging energetically at the soil with a trowel. Ann felt she mustn't go and lie down; William might come back and say she was lazy. He never had said anything like that, no matter how many times he caught her asleep on the sofa, but she hadn't forgotten how he had described herself and Gus as the idlest people he knew. Nor had she put from her mind his accusation that she had made him up. She thought it was possibly more accurate to say that

William had made *her* up; she certainly felt very unreal. She stayed awake until nine o'clock and fell asleep watching the television.

She woke at eleven and switched off the set. She looked at the food in the oven. The casserole had dried up, the potatoes fell like black stones onto the floor.

She waited a long time. There were all his clothes to sort out, his books. She sat on the windowsill in the bedroom and watched for his taxi to come down the hill.

At four o'clock she tiptoed downstairs and rang Edna. She dialed very softly, under the impression that maybe the telephone would ring less offensively at the other end. After a long time Edna answered. "Yes."

"I'm sorry. It's Ann. Is William there?"

"No, he isn't."

"I don't know what's happened to him."

"Surely you don't want sympathy from me," said Edna.

Ann started to make sniffling noises. She tried to control herself. "I'm sorry . . . I just thought . . ."

"It is final rehearsals," said Edna. "They don't keep civil service hours." And she put down the phone.

At eight o'clock William returned, white-faced and exhausted. He wore, unaccountably, corduroy trousers and a white sweater. Ann was on the landing stacking the pictures and the suitcase. He kissed her on the lips.

"Jesus," he said. "Have I had a time."

"Did the rehearsal go badly?" asked Ann. She did

her best to sound interested and reasonable.

"Get away," he said. "The rehearsal went fine. I had lunch with that bum, von Schreiber—"

"Chuck?" Ann said, severely.

"Aye, Chuck. We had snails at a place he knew in Wardour Street. I got toothache. I've never known such toothache. I went to a dentist."

"What dentist?" asked Ann.

"A bloke someone recommended. He gave me gas. When I came round he was hitting me in the face, he was belting me. And I vomited all over my breeches, down my coat and shirt, my socks, over the floor . . ."

"How awful," Ann said. She would have liked to look in his mouth for proof. She wondered if she could kiss him suddenly and feel with her tongue for any new fillings. But she couldn't bear to touch him.

"I had to buy new clothes," he went on. "The dentist threw my old ones away. I went back to rehearsal and I had a bath in Euston station. Andy put me to sleep on the set. I only woke up an hour ago." He yawned.

They piled everything into the van and sat on the front seat with the driver. Mrs. Kershaw didn't come out to say goodbye. The wardrobe remained in the hall. William put his arm round Ann and she couldn't thrust him away for fear he'd fall out of the door.

The new flat was in a Crescent not far from Regents Park—one large room and a small bedroom. There was a patio at the back, divided from the main yard, paved with slate, by a row of tubs planted with small bushes. The kitchen was in the living room and the bathroom was one flight up. Everything was painted white.

William hung his suits and jackets inside the built-in wardrobe; there was hardly room for Ann's blue smock and the unrestored coat. She couldn't help noticing his overcoat was missing, the tweed jacket, his silk dressing gown. From the front windows she could see the houses opposite, children playing on the pavement, the street lamps melting in a curve of steel over the camber of the road.

There was a surprise for her, he said, in the bedroom.

She felt she'd had enough surprises to last the rest of her life. Reluctantly she went to look. Braked against the wall was a pram in cream and chrome, the hood encased in polythene. It had a shopping basket at the foot.

"That's jolly useful," she said.

He put a packet of tea and his plimsolls in the shopping compartment and made her wheel it up and down the room.

She felt nothing at all. She was empty, absent. Blank.

He hadn't had time to buy any furniture. There weren't any chairs or a table. They drank tea and ate toast, sitting on suitcases at his desk. The pram stood with gleaming mudguards and white wheels at the centre of the white room. She breathed in and out, sat sedately on the suitcase buckling under her weight, munching her buttered toast.

He left for Newcastle the following day.

5

The play, though poorly attended, received good notices in the local press. William sent Ann copies of the papers. She didn't read them all through. Chuck von Schreiber had travelled up from London to see the play and seemed not such a bum after all.

William had decided to rewrite one of the scenes in the tenement, and cut out a scene towards the end where the boy was in a graveyard looking for the tomb of his mother. The mother must have died halfway through the play, she thought. She hadn't realised it was a tragedy.

He said there wasn't time to come back to London before they went on to Liverpool. She was to be patient and take her vitamins and he would send her the fare to Liverpool as soon as he was settled. In the meantime she should polish the furniture and wash the rugs and make her nest ready for the bairn. He loved her. He was her dulcimer boy. She didn't even bother to look the word up in the dictionary.

Clinical and bare, save for the desk, and the plates and cups on the draining board, the white room encircled her. She threw a blanket over the pram in the bedroom and sat for several hours a day in her fur coat on the patio looking at the row of shrubs. A woman in the upstairs flat called down once from her window. Ann pretended not to hear—she had been quite friendly with Mrs. Kershaw and look where that had landed her.

When William sent her the fare to Liverpool and a timetable of trains she could take, she was surprised. She hadn't thought he had meant her to come. She wrote and said it would be better if she stayed where she was. He sent a series of telegrams, expressing reproach and love. I NEED YOU. I LOVE YOU. WHAT IS WRONG? After some days she wrote again, in more detail; she said she couldn't come, feeling as she did. There were too many unexplained things. She didn't like mysteries. She knew she was odd and suspicious, but it seemed such a funny thing to have happened—being ill at the dentist's and losing all one's clothes, etc., etc. She had never known anyone before to whom that had happened. Surely the dentist had been overbearing to throw away the new jacket and trousers; he could have sent them to the cleaners. And what did William wear between the time he left the dentist's and bought the new corduroys?

William send a further telegram saying tersely, I NEED YOU. She didn't reply. She stayed indoors and thought of herself as a snaillike creature, similar to those under the leaves of the shrubs on the patio, curled within shells, motionless.

152

It was her mother who brought about the change. Mrs. Walton had telephoned Nethersole Road and been told by Mrs. Kershaw that Ann had left. There was no telephone number. She had then rung the BBC and was informed that Miss Walton had handed in her notice before Christmas. She wrote that she was disgusted at Ann's lack of decency. She had been given a wonderful education, a stable background; sacrifices had been made on her behalf —holidays, a larger car. She had no right to give up her job without first consulting her. All the years spent struggling to do without. God knows it hadn't been easy; there were things she could mention if only she was as selfish as Ann. The deceit was what hurt most of all. Ann owed her something—yes, owed. She demanded to know what Ann was up to.

The letter was such a tirade of pride and possessiveness that Ann was shaken. There was no mention of love or her father's health or the state of the garden and the Wine Society. There was no mention of anything but Mrs. Walton's divine right to be at the centre of the universe. The letter ended, "You foolish girl. Don't expect me to come running when your fancy man lets you down."

Ann put the letter on the floor. She walked into the bedroom and looked at the pram. She tore off the polythene hood and was amazed to see a small storm shield, with a square of plastic, through which, at some point in the future, when it rained, she would see her sleeping baby. She made breakfast, rocked the pram with one hand as she ate her toast. She looked at the timetable that William had sent her. If she went out now and bought some new clothes, she could be with him by supper time. She sent him a telegram at half past nine. CATCHING TWO O'CLOCK TRAIN. STOPPING AT CREWE. I LOVE YOU. YOUR FOOLISH GIRL.

She chose a grey tunic dress. She didn't look pregnant. Even sideways. It would go with her grey coat which still fitted her. She bought purple stockings and purple shoes of patent leather. She wanted to tell the shop assistant about William, how beautiful he was, how clever. She was terrified at the thought that she had nearly lost him.

She washed her hair and dried it sitting on the patio. She waved at the woman leaning out of the top window shaking a yellow duster. Only when she bent over her stomach to swing her head to and fro in the breeze did she catch her breath. The baby was taking up space beneath her ribs.

*

Everything about the journey she was determined to store up in her mind to remember for the rest of her life. Nothing must be forgotten—no detail of landscape or cluster of buildings glimpsed from the carriage window as she sped towards William. She would tell her baby about it, when it was a grown man or woman. Before you were born, she would say, we had a misunderstanding, your father and I, a parting. Then he sent for me to come to him, and I went to Euston in a new grey dress and boarded a train to the North.

She was so busy visualising the scene with the adult child, that she missed entirely the passage through the embankment, the slope of Primrose Hill, where William walked his children. Her own mother and father had never discussed those early days of love, the bombing days of wartime when Captain Walton enjoyed his life. She had never seen them kiss, touch hands, lie together in a bed. Only in photographs—the wedding picture, just the two of them: Captain Walton, his cap gripped beneath the biceps of his arm, and her mother smiling in a frock with square shoulders, her hair in a roll above her ears, a tilted hat—a little veil like a wisp of smoke—behind which the eyes stared out hungrily, glittering with gaiety. And another celluloid image of her parents on honeymoon, side by side on deck-chairs at Torquay, clutching each other, faces turned to the camera, smiling inscrutably with van-ished, slitted eyes. She hadn't any photographs of William to show the baby when it came.

She was aware of an old man, seated in the corner opposite, fast asleep with carefully composed limbs and a strawberry mark on his cheek. She needn't worry—it didn't happen anymore, that kind of blemish: if it did they scraped it off at once, as soon as the child was born.

The train slowed. Behind a hawthorn hedge a man rode a hefty horse down a lane. Plump and skittish, it swished its tail, dipped its head at the sound of the rolling wheels. She had never lived inland, away from the sea. She was travelling through an area of devastation, a rubbish tip of piebald fields filled with falling barns of rusty tin, chicken coops, lumpy cows lying down under a pale sky. How dirty they were, the cows, splattered with dried mud, sullenly munching. What a mess it was, the countryside, fractured and torn, threaded with abandoned canals, tyres floating along the thick green water—caravans, ruined cars, obsolete tractors, bushes ghostly with lime from a kiln ripped out of the ground; sheep, yellow and grazing, soaring on a strip of wet field, high into the air above the telegraph wires, as the train dipped downhill.

She would tell William that she hadn't meant to make demands. No matter how many times she failed to understand his manipulations, the devious routes he travelled, she wouldn't be possessive. He didn't owe her anything.

She remembered, as a child, being home for the holidays, and a friend of her father's calling to take her and her mother for a ride in a car. They stopped at a tea-shop in Lewes; they had cream cakes with jam leaking from the sides. The man, dapper and dark, removed the fox fur from her mother's shoulders. Her painted nails, like talons, curved the handle of the teapot; her rounded chin doubled as she gave that sharp and thrilling laugh. She kissed Ann repeatedly, she called her my own darling, she told the dapper man that she was the cleverest little girl in the world. When they went home, her mother took off her cheeky hat, her smile, her flowered dress. She stood grimly preparing the evening meal, the thin mouth fading as the scarlet lipstick wore away. Was that why she was so fierce when Ann mentioned this man or that—Gerald or William? Was she afraid that the cleverest little girl in the world might peel potatoes, all her life, for the wrong man?

156

The train leapt along the track, county to county. The fields flew, black and brown and tender mauve. "William, William, William" went the wheels on the steel rails above the cinders and the stones. Then another train, dark red and rocking, coming out of nowhere, rattling alongside the carriage—people drinking coffee, holding cups with both hands against the sway—gone again, left behind, swerving sideways into the distance. More fields, cut into furrows by the plough, glinting with strips of rainwater. A church set among juniper and laurel. Horses running, men chopping wood.

The train stopped at Wolverhampton. The old man woke up and unwrapped a cigar. The mark on his cheek was deep purple. William had a mole on his back, below his shoulder blade. When he smiled the edges of his teeth showed. The enamel was thin. He said it was to do with a lack of calcium as a child. Same with his feet. Neglected. The toes curled inwards like claws, the fault of the cheap footwear passed on from Charlie Clintoch, Andrew Baines and the boy two flights up in the tenement whose name he had forgotten.

She wished she had brought the newspapers he had sent her. She should have read his reviews. But he would understand, surely, when she told him how cold she had gone inside, how resentful. It showed a certain kind of love, even if it was the wrong kind.

The train left the station, out into a wasteland of freight yards and sidings. You see, William, she explained in her head, I was so suspicious of you that

I couldn't believe you'd gone to the dentist and been ill. I know it sounds silly.

She didn't really think it was silly, even now. It still nagged in her mind, that business of the thrown-away clothes and the naked journey to the rehearsal rooms.

Gardens slid past the window—allotments, fences made of doors, shacks of corrugated iron, potting sheds, greenhouses with smashed panes of glass, two women tossing cabbages into a tall and battered pram.

She'd never thanked him for the pram. And she'd hurt him, she knew, when she'd sent Pamela away, that she should be so uncharitable. The holiday he wanted to give them—how happy he'd been showing his brochures, talking about Barcelona in the mild wintertime. And she'd stopped him. All the same, deep down she was glad it had come to nothing.

The old man in the corner was dozing again; the cigar hung from his lip. It was odd how, at both ends of life, people slept in the day. Her father napped in the morning and in the afternoon. Quite suddenly his eyes, scanning the newspaper or the military book, would close, his head slip sideways, his jaw slacken: as if he had been overcome by gas. When he went to bed he complained of waking before dawn. Dentists gave gas for extractions . . . sometimes . . . William hadn't said he'd lost a tooth . . . Pamela was a dental receptionist. . . .

The day brightened. The thick white sky broke up into clouds threaded with blue. She could hardly keep her eyes open. When she awoke, her nose hurt. She had been lying with it pressed to the window. She rubbed her face. All through her childhood, her mother had stroked her nose downwards, before brushing her hair. "Believe me," she had said. "A straight nose is an asset to a girl." It had worked, though perhaps a little too well. Nobody had worried about William's assets. The baby, for sure, would have a button of a nose.

The old man in the corner was awake, relighting the stump of his cigar. She asked him whether they were near Liverpool yet. He stared at her disapprovingly, as if she had importuned him. Perhaps he was deaf. She looked out of the window. There were poplars along the horizon and pale fields of green grass. Gone in a flash, replaced by buildings and blackened walls. A signal box. The beginnings of a station—was it Liverpool? She leapt up at once, eager to read the name on the white-painted board. Crewe. She was disappointed that she wasn't at journey's end. She went to the toilet to wash her hands and comb her hair. She would have liked to use the lavatory but she knew it wasn't allowed when the train was halted. Suddenly she remembered Uncle Walter singing about a porter who wanted to go to Birmingham. Humming, she went back along the corridor. The train was now filled with passengers. It took her several minutes to reach her seat. The old man had taken her suitcase down to secure her place. "Thank you," she said. He pretended not to hear. A whistle blew. The guard waved a green flag on the platform. The train moved on. She watched the people in the carriage with interest: a woman with two children, a commercial traveller, case of samples on his knee, a merchant navy man in a shiny brown suit, pin-striped. He had something blue, like a flower or a badge, tattooed on the back of his hand. She prided herself on being observant. There was a constant flow of people passing down the corridor, looking for somewhere to sit. There was a woman in trou-sers, ducking her head to see if the empty seat was reserved. A man followed her, dressed in a blue dufflecoat and wearing sunglasses. It was William. He passed her by. She let him go. She felt foolish.

"William," she called, standing up and looking after him.

He turned and came towards her. He took her in his arms and kissed her. He pushed his knee be-tween her legs, his tongue right into her mouth. She pulled away from him. She was worried in case he behaved as he had done in the hospital. The old man was watching her.

"Why are you here?" she asked.

"I could'na wait."

He took off his sunglasses and his eyes were red-rimmed, as they had been all that time ago when he had gone swimming at Swiss Cottage.

"I do love you," she told him, swaying against him, clinging to his warm blue coat.

"Ahhh," he went, loud above the rattle of the carriage. He leaned sideways, reaching with his hand to steady himself on the web of the luggage rack. He pulled the communication cord. The old man saw him—Ann saw, nobody else. She wouldn't have noticed if she hadn't seen his fingers dragging on the little metal chain. After a minute the train began to decelerate.

"Oh William," she said. "What will we do?"

She stared out at the fields that were slowing down—cuts of oak and beech and chestnut in a timber yard, rotting in the damp air. There was a long drawn out groan as the train came to a standstill. People read newspapers. The children whined and scrabbled on the dusty floor for dropped crayons. The old man looked steadfastly at William, the butt of his cigar clamped in his mouth like a dummy. The guard came in his suit of blue serge. He had his notebook ready.

"Now then," he said, like a policeman in a pantomime. "Who done it and why?"

Ann giggled. William took two five-pound notes out of his wallet, white and folded like pocket handkerchiefs.

"I want to get off," he said.

He gave his name and address, though Ann couldn't hear it, because her face was burning, her heart thumping. She wished the old man would stop staring.

The guard said William hadn't heard the last of it. He unfolded the five-pound notes and held them up to the light. William said he didn't mind. If that was all, he was getting off now. He pushed Ann in front of him, carrying her suitcase. She stumbled past the outstretched feet, the crawling children. He opened the door. Below, the track was covered in pebbles, like the beach at home. He jumped onto the stones, held out his arms. Ann hesitated. The guard stood outraged behind her. She stepped down, and William lifted her onto the grass verge and pulled her up a small bank into a field. He put his arm round her. He swung her suitcase into the air and laughed. They plodded over the grass towards a clump of elms, grey as smoke, and a road beyond. Her patent-leather shoes filled slowly with mud. She looked back at the train, still stationary, the blurred faces at the windows of the carriages.

"Where are we?" she asked, floundering over the marshy field, her stockings splashed with dirt.

"Cheshire," he told her, lifting her almost off her feet, kissing her cheek whipped by the wind.

He stopped a car on the main road and asked for a lift. The driver and his wife were going into Crewe to visit their son-in-law; he was something quite big in the timber trade.

"Well, he's only just started, like," admitted the proud Mother-in-law. "But it's early days."

William said he had been let down by a car-hire firm. They were newlyweds and they had a room booked at the Crewe Arms Hotel. The man grunted; the wife shifted on her seat and sighed.

The hotel was three miles away, opposite the station. It stood like a prison, built of brick and stone, blackened by the coal dust from the steam trains.

"Thanks awfully," said Ann, deposited on the pavement with suitcase and bridegroom.

They walked down a flight of steps railed in wrought iron, waved to the couple in the car, went into the revolving doors, spun round and out onto a purple carpet whorled with flowers.

William said he couldn't bear her to come to

Liverpool. He had gone to Crewe to prevent her. He couldn't find her when the train stopped.

"I was in the loo," she said.

He didn't want her to see the play. It was absurd, trivial; she was the only thing that counted. A flower, a Michaelmas daisy. He wanted them to be here, in the middle of nowhere, together, to recapture their love, which was beyond price—or first nights of plays, or futile men and women calling each other darling. "You're my darling," he said. "My ain folk." And his eyes filled with tears, and she comforted him, saying over and over he was her sweetheart, her dulcimer boy.

She preened herself in the dining room, sure of him, eating her sardine salad, her loin of pork. The carpeting was so thick, they talked in whispers.

"They want the play in America."

"Oh good. That is good."

"It doesn't matter. You're what matters."

"I love you—"

"They may not want it in the end—"

"Oh, they will, they will."

"It's early days."

"When you go to America," she said.

"When *we* go to America," he corrected.

"We'll have to take the baby."

"Aye," he said. "We'll have to take the bairn."

He put down his knife and fork. He stretched out his hands across the table and cradled her face. It was unbearable how much they loved each other.

There was an elderly cashier seated at a desk by the door. She had a little gold pencil hanging by a chain from her spectacles. William thanked her for the meal. She simpered and jerked her head. The little pencil swung back and forth beneath her withered ear.

It was like the beginning, before it got spoilt. He didn't hold her like a wheelbarrow at the side of the bed, arch her back, shout the crude words. He was tender, gentle, life-enhancing. He tried to explain how he had felt the last few dreadful weeks. The strain of his play . . . events growing beyond his control. At home the consistent critic, the patient misunderstander . . . arranging life a little better than he liked it . . . preferring not quite the same things as himself . . . turning the past over and over. Endeavouring not to poke the eyes of the cat with a pencil, but to stroke its ears. She didn't understand any of it. It sounded as if he was criticising her, or was he talking about Edna? She daren't dwell on the bit about the cat.

He said of all the people in the world she was dearest to his heart—his little baby-maker, the one who believed him, whose capacity for deception was as great as his own.

She only partially understood him. She had to struggle to clear his words from the layers beneath. She thought there shouldn't be any other people to choose from—there weren't for her: he'd blotted out the sun. And he'd had babies before, by Sheila. She choked back the questions, the demands. "Oh I do love you," she repeated, over and over.

In the morning she enjoyed her eggs-and-bacon, the slices of thin toast, the sticky lump of marmalade in the dish. She closed her eyes to the H.P. sauce he poured onto his plate.

"Isn't this nice," she said.

"Aye," he agreed. She must go home on the morning train—no, she must. He would follow on the midnight. He'd be home tomorrow morning in time for breakfast. He had to be off again to Glasgow in a few days—he frowned at her dejected face. Not for long: then never, never, never would they be separated again.

"I'll make you sick of me," he boasted. "You'll see."

"I won't be sick," she said.

"Jesus," he said wonderingly, "We've almost cracked it, haven't we?"

"Ssshh," she admonished. "People are looking."

But he was right, she thought. They had cracked it.

He put her on the train to London. He kissed her in the carriage doorway. He said the most beautiful things. I want . . . I need . . . I love . . .

Out went the train, a reversal of yesterday—the same sidings, the same trees, sheep, muddy cows. Backwards, away from him, unphotographed, unrecorded, jumbled in the memory.

*

When she arrived at the flat, she was worn out. She slept late into the evening. Then she bathed, washed her hair, tried to make the room look like home, for William. She hadn't any nails to hammer into the walls, so she perched his pictures on the shelf above the cooker. She parked the pram by the doors leading onto the patio and searched in her suitcase for the half-finished garment he had made for the baby. She laid it on the waterproof cover of the pram. If only she had furnished the room for him. She flushed her mother's letter down the lavatory.

When the doorbell rang at midnight, she was eating a cheese sandwich. She ran to the door thinking it was William come on an earlier train. It was Edna. There wasn't time to hide the pram. It stood there like an expensive toy. Edna didn't look sad or agitated. She was smiling as if it were a social call.

She said, "I felt compelled to come."

She had a lot of thin scarves, made out of gauze, tied about her throat. When she took off her coat of beaver lamb, she was wearing a satin garment without sleeves; it could have been a nightdress, or a thin frock meant for dancing.

"Is everything all right?" asked Ann, putting the sandwich down on the draining board, and taking the coat into the bedroom.

"No," said Edna. "He promised he wouldn't move. Why is his desk here?"

"We live here," Ann said.

There was nothing for Edna to sit on. She walked about the room, the gauze scarves floating above her bare shoulders. There was a straggle of hair, like wire, frizzed at the pit of her arm. "Why did you come here in the first place?" she asked.

Ann told her about the roof and her landlady wanting the ceiling taken down. "So William found another flat," she said. "With a garden."

Edna said, "William told me he had a fight with someone called Roddy. Mrs. Kershaw asked him to leave. You were embarrassed. He said it was only fair to find you a new place before he came home."

"But he's not going home," said Ann. "He can't."

"It was never a permanent relationship," said Edna. "You knew that."

"It's jolly well got to be," Ann said. "I'm having a baby."

"You're young," Edna observed. "Do you like the pram? I bought it at John Barnes."

After some seconds Ann began to cry. When she was able, she said, "I don't understand any of you. I've just been to Liverpool to see William. We were so happy."

"To Liverpool?" said Edna. "William said you wouldn't go. He said it was over."

"Well, it isn't," said Ann. "I did go."

It was Edna's turn to be distressed. The thought of Ann in Liverpool with William was obviously unbearable to her. "But Pamela's there," she said. "She went three days ago. After that, he said he was coming home to me. I only permitted it on those grounds."

I don't believe any of it, thought Ann. But she did.

They both began to pace the room—Ann, lost and fearful, dragging her feet. Edna skimming across the bare linoleum in her ballet slippers. They passed each other several times with despairing eyes and faces wet with tears.

"Does he go to bed with you?" asked Ann, finally.

"I'm his wife," said Edna.

Ann sat down on the floor with her back to the wall. She covered her face with her hands. "Why does he do it?" she said. "I was perfectly happy. I was going to marry Gerald."

Edna didn't reply. She was squatting beside the pram, muscular thighs bulging beneath the satin nightdress, checking the brakes, the quality of the canvas hood. The tears ran down her cheeks.

"But why?" repeated Ann. "Why did he have to send for Pamela?"

"He doesn't believe in free fall," Edna said. "He won't let go of the branch until he's quite sure of the next one." She wiped her eyes with her fist.

"He must be ill," moaned Ann. "All the things he said. All those words. When I got your letter, he said not to take any notice. I felt awful. I really did. That bit about you feeling you were in prison—"

"Yes," said Edna. "William thought that might get through to you." She rubbed her bare arms, teetered on her heels. She said severely, "I never wanted to write it. It seemed to me like blackmail. It's not my style at all. But William dictated it . . . he said it was for the best."

They stared at each other—Ann against the wall, skinny and hunched, Edna fleshy in the peach-coloured nightdress. They were like rodents on the floor of a cage, dwarfed under the ceiling.

Edna talked about William.

Ann didn't want to listen, but what else could she do? If she allowed her mind to wander, she was faced with snapshots, one after the other: a field outside Crewe, Pamela on the divan with the silver coins round her neck, Mrs. Kershaw motionless in the pink bedroom, Edna lying down in wifely fashion, ballet slippers flung at the foot of a chair.

Edna said William had a high IQ. His father drank: sometimes they took his trumpet from him by force and covered him with a coat in a doorway. Sheila had torn up William's scripts, burned his first new suit in the back yard. He had left for London with Gus, had paid for him to go to night school. William and Edna had spent some time in a cottage near Merthyr Tydfil with the children. Sheila had gone off to Spain with a waiter she'd met in Shepherds Bush. William cut logs, dragged pails of water from the river. He found a swallow with a broken wing, nursed it, caught insects for it from the air, killed it with overfeeding. Sheila often came to visit Edna. She had arrived some weeks ago after seeing William in a taxi with a girl; he had said he was in Manchester that week and couldn't visit the children. Sheila ran beside the taxi until it turned to go down the hill and a Bentley ran into it. You could hear the impact quite plainly. Sheila hoped he had broken his neck. She couldn't make sure because she had to collect the children from school. But then Sheila was vindictive; she didn't understand William. He was a beautiful person. For all his compartments, he was undeniably a golden boy.

Outside it grew light. There was a roll of swollen cloud, red above the rooftops. Edna faded, became grey and tired. Ann lay slumped on the floor.

The golden boy returned at seven o'clock. If he was surprised at seeing the two of them together, he hid it. He hesitated on the threshold of the unfurnished room. Whom should he embrace first? He kissed Edna, touched the breast of her nightdress, bent towards Ann cowering on the floor. She thought she might be sick.

"William," said Edna. "You have to give some answers."

Ann waited to hear the questions.

William lay down on the white squares of linoleum. He cupped his hands under his head and closed his eyes.

"Are you going to stay here, living with Ann?"

"Yes."

"You don't intend to come back home?"

"No."

Ann wanted to ask what Pamela had been doing in Liverpool. But she knew. Instead she whispered into the crook of her arm "Do you love me?"

"Yes."

"Do you want a divorce then?" asked Edna.

"No," said William.

*

Ann knew she must go straight back to Nethersole Road and never see William again. She mustn't let him through the door. She would change the locks, bar the windows. When Edna had gone, she screamed and shouted at him. She thought that if she made enough noise she wouldn't hear what he said. He wouldn't be able to confuse her and make her feel she had imagined it all. She threw his pictures from the shelf and jumped up and down on them.

"Don't do that," he said. "You'll break the glass."
He said he could explain everything, if only she
would empty her mind of pride and ownership.
Love was all that counted. He was here, wasn't he?

"Be quiet," she screamed.

Why, he persisted, was he here, if he didn't need
to be?

"God knows," she raged. "Maybe Pamela thinks
you've popped out to the dentist. Or you're looking
at graveyards."

"Don't talk like that," he said, as if she uttered
obscenities. "I'm here because I want to be. Can't
you see that?" He seemed genuinely puzzled.

"No, I can't," she cried. "I don't think you know
where you are. There's so many of us, you've got
confused."

She was thinking of Pamela. The thought that
Pamela had been in Liverpool made her want to kill
him.

He said cunningly, "You left me to go home to
your mother. You let me be on my own."

She sprang at him. She beat at his chest with her
fists.

"Go away," she said. "Get away from me."

He bore the blows stoically; he watched her with
sad forgiving eyes. He refused to budge.

"Very well," she cried. "You stay." And she ran
out of the house not bothering to close the door. It
was raining and she was without her shoes.

She phoned Mrs. Kershaw from a box in the next
street. "I want to come back," she said. "I have to
come back."

"There's the roof," said Mrs. Kershaw.

Ann said sternly, "There's nothing wrong with the roof."

"It's damaged," Mrs. Kershaw insisted.

"I can't answer for what may happen if you don't let me have my flat back. It's terribly important."

"I'll let you know," said Mrs. Kershaw.

"I have to know now."

"Well, I can't tell you right away. I'm going up north in a few days' time and I'm rather busy at the moment. Naturally, I'll have to talk to Roddy."

William had left when Ann returned. He had taken with him his picture of Dennis Law.

"Good riddance," she shouted triumphantly, squelching about the room in her saturated stockings, a brave smile on her lips.

She didn't wait for Mrs. Kershaw to talk to Roddy. She visited her that afternoon. She told her what had happened—the train, Pamela, Edna, the nightly rides that were never in the direction of his children. Mrs. Kershaw was appalled. She didn't say much, but the roses left her cheeks; even her lips turned pale. In one sense, thought Ann, Mrs. Kershaw was partly to blame. If she hadn't been so free with her bicycle, William might never have had the energy to make so many contacts.

6

It was such a relief to be back in Nethersole Road that Ann was almost happy—for a short while, a matter of days. His desk had gone, those beautiful shirts in the wardrobe, the bunches of socks, the folded handkerchiefs. Even the nights lying in the double bed proved not to be such an ordeal as she had feared. It was only a bed. It had existed before she had known him, had accommodated Douglas from the BBC and Gerald. It wasn't exclusive to William. So she told herself.

Mrs. Kershaw didn't go up North. She said the children objected to being left with Roddy. Ann offered to help, but Mrs. Kershaw said she'd changed her mind. She didn't want to go any more. She seemed subdued, less buoyant. Her feet went flat-footedly over the gravel to the bins. She put the bicycle in the back garden, as if out to grass.

She was good to Ann. She came upstairs of an evening to keep her company. She began to make

173

a little mug for the baby, glazed in blue. She thought it was better for Ann to discuss her problems, instead of bottling them up inside. Why did Ann think William had told his wife about her in the first place? What had he said in the hotel in Crewe? When did she first suspect that he was seeing Pamela? Mrs. Kershaw probed. She questioned.

"At the beginning, did he seem sincere?"

"Terribly," said Ann. "Oh, he was terribly sincere. At least, that first week."

"But then," said Mrs. Kershaw, "you said he never went out."

"Yes," admitted Ann. "Well, except, you know? to visit the children."

"But he didn't visit them, did he?"

"Oh, he did," she cried defensively. "Not every night I grant you, but he did sometimes." She felt spiteful towards Mrs. Kershaw. "That bicycle of yours," she said with a rueful smile, trying to make a joke of it.

"Yes," said Mrs. Kershaw dully. "That bloody bike."

It destroyed Ann's calm, the nightly interrogations. The dreams began again, the waving from departure bays. She woke in the night calling his name. She heard Edna asking him if he wanted a divorce. Her heart beat loudly. She waited. The cars went by. William said no. She put her hands fearfully upon her stomach. She was never going to be a wife but undoubtedly she was going to be a mother. What was going to happen to her? How would she manage? She thought she would try to get her old job back at the BBC. She could tell them she had left to be married.

When she received her bank statement, she was astonished to find it had been credited with three hundred pounds. It could only have been William. Did it mean he loved her?

She rang Edna. No, Edna hadn't seen him for some days, but then he was up north in Glasgow. He was quite alone. Pamela was on holiday in Barcelona. The play was due to come on in the West End in August.

"He's put money in my bank," said Ann.

"Aye," Edna said. "He's very good with money."

After some thought, Ann wrote to Gerald. She said—

If I hurt you, you will be pleased to know that I am being punished for it. That man I told you of, has left me and I am having a baby. It seems a long time ago since I said goodbye to you. We did have pleasant times, didn't we?

She didn't know his University address, so she sent it to his old employers, the architects' firm in Kensington. She asked them to forward it.

She waited daily for a reply, but none came.

The wardrobe still blocked out the light in the hall—the mahogany folk-singing chamber with the brass handles. She tried to look inside but someone had locked the doors. Somebody, Roddy possibly, had written in chalk across the front. "Move this bloody monstrosity." When she passed it to go shopping, she touched the grained wood fleetingly with her hand.

One morning, descending the green carpeted stairs in her dressing gown, she saw the cream perambulator parked in the hall. There was a single cut flower, a hothouse rose, on the waterproof cover. She ran down the last flight of steps. She rummaged inside the hood for a note, a message. There was nothing. She knocked at Mrs. Kershaw's door. Roddy answered. He held a newspaper in front of his naked body.

"Is Mrs. Kershaw in?" she asked, ignoring his smooth chest, his hairy legs.

"No," he said rudely, slamming the door in her face.

She took the rose upstairs and cried over it. She pried the petals apart, searching for a sign.

Mrs. Kershaw came upstairs at midday. She had found an envelope jammed in the flap of the letter box.

"It's from him," said Ann. "I know it."

"You'll have to do something about that bloody pram," said Mrs. Kershaw. "Roddy's livid."

The note said, "Please for the love of God, let me back. I want to be with you and my bairn."

"Don't fall for that," said Mrs. Kershaw violently. "He'll only upset you."

She strode about the living room in her sandals and her cotton blouse. She wore her short hair curled like a gypsy, and hoops of brass in her ears.

"Of course I won't," said Ann. She wished Mrs. Kershaw would go away so that she could read the few lines he had written, over and over.

He knocked at her door at two o'clock in the morning. Ann had changed the locks and his key wouldn't fit. He stood like a bashful boy, penitent, hanging his head.

"I'll not bother you," he said, mock modest. "Unless you want me back."

She was so happy she forgot Mrs. Kershaw's advice, her own good sense. She nestled into his arms. She took him in without a word of reproach. Back went the bundles of socks into the wardrobe, the collection of shirts.

He was a reformed character. If the telephone rang, he took her by the hand and went down with her into the hall. He forced her to hear his conversations, the appointments, the invitations to lunch and dinner. He showed her the letters he received. He was never late home. Neither of them mentioned Edna or Pamela. She told him she had written to Gerald.

"Ah well," he said. "I canna blame you. It's natural enough." His eyes, it seemed, had become a deeper shade of blue, full of candour and friendliness.

"What did you mean?" she asked. "About the cat?"

"What cat?"

"The cat you talked about that dreadful night we were in Crewe."

"Is that how you remember it?" he said, hurt. "Was it dreadful to you?"

She felt ashamed. She was constantly letting him down. It had been the following night, of course, that had been so painful.

He asked Chuck von Schreiber for supper. He was tall, with a moustache, and he brought Ann a box of chocolates. She didn't like him. He looked at William as if they shared secrets. He wore a silver ring on his little finger. He put his arm about William's shoulders frequently. He never lost an opportunity to touch him, brush against him in some way, hand or knee, as he told an anecdote about an outing in Newcastle . . . Liverpool . . .

"Ah, Chuck," said William. "Leave it be."

"What's he doing here?" Ann snapped, slapping the dishes into the sink, making the coffee. "Why doesn't he go home to America?"

"He's my mate," said William. "He's not as important as you. But he counts. Don't misunderstand that. He does count."

"Well, he can count right out of here," she said in a fury. "Get him out of here."

She made coffee. She poured it out. She was quite amusing about her experiences at the BBC. William sang. Chuck joined in. Ann put her finger beneath her ear, as she had seen on television, and attempted to harmonise.

"Jesus," said William. "You're tone deaf, Ann."

She fell silent. She sulked. She went into the bedroom and left them together. Her voice wasn't that bad; as a junior she had been in the school choir.

There was laughter from the sitting room—movement. William came into the bedroom. She pretended to be asleep. He took things from the wardrobe. Later she heard him go downstairs with Chuck. She thought they were saying goodnight. She peeped out of the window, but the hedge hid the car from view. She waited for William's foot-steps on the stair. He never came back. She was sorry then she had been so rude to his friend, so critical. She leant against the wardrobe, empty of his shirts and socks and cried. She cried on and off for several days.

"But what did you say?" asked Mrs. Kershaw, mystified.

"Nothing," said Ann. "I was a bit nasty to Chuck."

"Well, what did William say, then?"

"Nothing," said Ann. "Except that I was tone deaf."

Ann pushed the pram out onto the gravel and left it by the bins. She hoped someone would steal it. The next day it was back in the hall.

Gerald replied to her letter.

I find it very difficult to understand. I have heard nothing from you. You did not reply to my letters. Imagine my distress when your letter came this morning. I have told everyone about you. I will come back to England in June to see you. This will be expensive but I feel it is worth it. I think we should get married. I don't care about the baby. I am shocked that such a thing should have happened so soon after I left. However I reckon we can both overcome this obstacle if we are sensible. I have sent 300 dollars to your bank on the Finchley Road. Keep your chin up. Gerald.

"What on earth will my bank manager think?" she asked Mrs. Kershaw. "All those men sending me money." And she laughed and stood vulgarly with her stomach thrust forward, her face round with health.

"I thought you said Gerald was cautious," said Mrs. Kershaw. "It's bloody noble of him wanting to marry you."

Ann rang Edna and told her of the latest developments—William leaving, Gerald's offer of marriage. Edna said she hadn't seen William for several days, though he had sent his shirts through the post for her to wash.

"I'd burn them," Ann said boldly.

But later, in the night, in the early morning, when she could swear she heard a nightingale singing in the trees beyond her window, she wept.

*

William came back, once in April and twice in May. On each occasion his arrival was dramatic and unannounced. In April, he broke into the flat when she was out shopping, splintering the jamb of the door and causing Roddy to send him a solicitor's letter. He was doing the washing up when she returned. He said for his own sake she must take him back. The second time he said it was for the sake of the child. Lastly, for Ann's sake. His clothing went in and out of her wardrobe. The pictures of Dennis Law and Samuel Palmer were never replaced on their hooks upon the wall; they stood stacked against the skirting board, ready for a quick getaway. It was the abrupt removal of the more mundane socks and handkerchiefs that caused her the most despair. Their disappearance never failed to break her heart into pieces.

In May, when he had come back with flowers in his hand and a folding bath for the baby, he left after a discussion about Catherine.

"I want Catherine to have liberty," he said. "I want her to be free."

"Catherine who?" she asked, baffled.

"My daughter," he said. "I want her to be happy."

"She'll go to University," Ann said. "She'll ask questions, she'll know about things . . . about people . . . about painters."

"Rubbish," he cried. "Just as long as she holds her head tall and her shoulders back."

He was saying that she, Ann, was round-shouldered. Her eyes smarted in the darkness.

"Pff," she said scornfully. "I don't care what she looks like. It's her brain that counts."

"You're daft," he said. "Who wants a woman for her brains?"

"Gerald would," she retorted. "He's not prejudiced."

Up jumped William from the bed. He went to the wardrobe, lifted out the coat hangers hung with suits, stuffed his socks into a carrier bag and leaped out onto the landing and down the stairs. She heard the sound of his plimsolls on the gravel path. His departures usually coincided with some letter or telegram arrived earlier in the day. She was not actually surprised, only devastated.

She tried to ring Edna, but she was either away or not answering her phone. If she had known how to

contact Sheila, she would have done. She felt his
wives and herself were citizens of some special
country. They knew about the frontiers, the trea-
ties. Anybody else would boggle at the absurdity of
the customs, the complexities of the language.

Each day, the postman brought parcels addressed
to Miss Catherine McClusky—items of clothing, a
shawl, even a teddy bear. The vests and the booties
and the little pink frocks waited where once William
had stored his handkerchiefs. She could hardly bear
to touch the small trousseau. She didn't want to
think about the birth. She felt it could never happen, or if it did, it would happen to someone else.
When Gerald comes, she promised herself, then I'll
think about the baby. Her doctor said she was a
healthy young woman—heart, urine, blood pressure, everything normal. Not my heart, she thought.
Surely my heart's not normal.

At the beginning of June she looked at herself in
Mrs. Kershaw's full-length mirror. It was very no-
ticeable from the side, her condition, but she wasn't
too bulky at the front.

"It won't go away," said Mrs. Kershaw. "Just by
looking at it."

"Is it very obvious?"

"Very," said Mrs. Kershaw.

"William sent me a new dress," said Ann. "A
pregnancy dress to get married in. It's green, with
little flowers."

"He thinks of everything," remarked Mrs. Kershaw dryly.

Two days before she expected him, Gerald cabled

Ann. She puzzled over it. PERHAPS IT IS FOR BEST. HOPE HE LOOKS AFTER YOU. GERALD.

She read it several times before taking it to show Mrs. Kershaw. The french windows were open and the children ran about the garden.

"I don't understand it," she said. "Do you?"

"Are you sure it's from him?" said Mrs. Kershaw. "Maybe it's a trick. Maybe William sent it."

They looked carefully at the despatching address and the date. It seemed genuine.

"Does it mean he's not coming?" said Ann.

"Did he have a sense of humour?" asked Mrs. Kershaw.

"No," Ann said.

Jasper came in wanting bread and jam. He ignored Ann. Mrs. Kershaw cut a slice from a brown wholemeal loaf. She had been gardening and dirt rimmed her nails.

"But why should he change his mind?" asked Ann.

"Why can't we have decent bread?" complained Jasper. He threw his sandwich on the floor.

"Pick that up," commanded Mrs. Kershaw.

"I don't want butter, only jam."

"It sounds as if someone's changed it for him," said Mrs. Kershaw.

She cut more bread and told Jasper to go outside. He wouldn't.

"How am I going to manage?" asked Ann pathetically. She still thought of herself as frail and skinny. Tubby and cumbersome, she lumbered about the room, feet splayed outwards to balance her weight. Jasper prodded her stomach.

"Don't," reproved his mother. "You'll hurt the baby."

"Silly," said Jasper. "It's in a bag of jelly. It can't feel anything."

He swung backwards and forwards against the handles of the french windows. The hinges creaked.

"Perhaps William will come back again," said Ann. She wondered if he was still bothered by free fall. Or had he found another branch to cling to? She said, "My mother's coming next week."

"You didn't ask her to come up for the wedding?" Mrs. Kershaw was shocked.

"I never asked her to come at all," said Ann. "She doesn't know about Gerald. Do you think you could come up sometimes and talk to her—flatter her—"

"How?" asked Mrs. Kershaw dubiously. She was struggling at the window with Jasper, trying to push him out into the garden.

"Tell her she looks pretty. She'll like that."

"Well," said Mrs. Kershaw evasively, "I'll talk to her."

Jasper stamped on her foot. She hit him over the head. He ran screaming onto the grass and hurled his jam sandwich into the rose bushes.

*

Mrs. Walton arrived, gay and summery, in a white coat and white gloves. She wore a hat made of navy straw, shaped like a basin, crammed with cloth roses. She laughed all the way up the stairs.

"What a lovely hat," called Ann, waiting for her

on the landing. Being near-sighted, her mother, at this distance, would not notice the change in her shape. Even in the hallway she seemed not to be aware of Ann's increase in size. Having put her suitcase in the bedroom and taken off her hat and coat, she came through into the kitchen. She was very controlled, very subtle. She said Ann looked well.

"Is that all?" asked Ann. She had developed a certain irony of manner as her body puffed out, her time grew near.

Her mother sat at the table. She helped herself to a chocolate digestive. Her eyes were moist and wary. She took a tissue out of her handbag and wiped the tear from her eye, the crumbs from her mouth. She was brave and practical. She asked, "What are you going to do?"

Ann wondered who had prepared her for the shock. Maybe Mrs. Kershaw had written to warn her, in case she had a heart attack on the spot. Perhaps she had done all her raging at home.

"Do?" she said.

"Do," repeated her mother.

"Get on with it," said Ann. "It's too late to do anything else." She took a biscuit.

Voice beginning to rise in pitch, her mother said, "His wife should be told."

"She has been," Ann said. "She thinks William's a beautiful person."

"Shooting's too good for him," said her mother shrilly. It was as if she'd promised herself, or someone else, that she would not shout recriminations at Ann and was now relieved that there were others on whom she could vent her feelings. "We must go to a solicitor. There should be financial arrangements. He mustn't be allowed to get off scot free."

"There are financial arrangements," said Ann. "He puts money in the bank. So does Gerald for that matter. He says he's coming to marry me."

"Marry you? Gerald?"

"Well, there's been some sort of delay. But he did send me money."

"You do surprise me," said her mother. "I can't say I took to him. Too dark . . . a touch of the Jew, if you ask me."

"Rubbish," said Ann. "He's Celtic. He comes from Devon."

Curiously, her mother wanted to know what she felt for William—not how it had happened or where he went to school, nothing about the General, but did they like the same things, share the same interests?

"I don't want to think about it," said Ann. "It hurts."

She couldn't talk to her mother about love. She suspected in any case that her mother's mood might evaporate fairly soon, and then she would regret her confidences. It was strange that she had been so scathing about Gerald. He hadn't been married twice or put Ann in the family way.

"When is it due?" asked her mother.

"I don't know," said Ann. "He was coming last week."

Her mother became alarmed. "Last week?"

Ann realised she meant the baby. "Next month," she said. "The pram's in the hall."

"What about a layette for the poor little thing?"

"There's masses of clothes in the wardrobe," said Ann. She didn't think of the baby as a poor little thing. It would be bouncing and deceitful, with a head of yellow curls. Her mother would have a job trying to straighten the little blob of a nose.

Mrs. Walton was oohing and aahing in the bedroom. She shouted, "Some of these little frocks are perfectly sweet. Where did you buy them?"

"I didn't," called Ann. "He did. Or probably his wife."

She was secretly astonished at the way her mother was behaving. Not one word yet of reproach. Not once had she called her a foolish girl. For her own part, she wasn't frightened of her any more. Even if she did start labelling her slut, prostitute, gold-digger, she didn't think it would affect her greatly. After all, she thought, we are both mothers now. More or less.

Mrs. Walton tried hard to remain tolerant. She didn't ask for cups of tea to be brought to her. She slept in the double bed, but she gave Ann one of her pillows to supplement those on the divan. She even cooked little meals for her. She did the shopping. Considering she had left behind her bridge parties and her Wine Society, she was very patient. Ann wouldn't go out. Only into the back garden. Her mother didn't know, but it was because Ann didn't want William to see them together. If he happened to glimpse them in the street, linking arms, he would think she was being looked after and he would never come back.

Her mother walked her round the badminton court and admired Mrs. Kershaw's roses. She saw

Jasper playing with a black boy on the grass.

"Doesn't he have any normal little friends?" she asked, laughing gaily in the direction of the children, fluttering her white glove in greeting.

She had several long chats with Mrs. Kershaw, when Ann was resting in the bedroom. Sometimes she was irritable afterwards. She tossed her head viciously remarking, "My word, times have changed. She admitted that person came to live here with her consent."

"She's a good friend to me," said Ann.

Mrs. Walton couldn't deny it. She couldn't afford to be critical. How dreadful if Mrs. Kershaw, on moral grounds, had turned Ann out into the street and she had been forced to go home to Brighton. In her condition. She said, "I've never seen her husband. Is she a widow?"

"No," said Ann. "She's got a friend."

"I see," said her mother, tight-lipped.

"She has been married," Ann ventured. "Twice in fact."

"Oh," said her mother, amazed. "She's not backward in coming forward, then?"

It was to her credit that she kept her temper in check, held back the bitter words. It was very difficult for her, under the circumstances. All those years of duty and conformity gone for nothing. Of no value. Twenty years later the old standards swept away as if they had never been. There was Ann, pregnant, unmarried, money in the bank, neither ostracised nor selling heather in the gutter. Unrepentant. One might say, unaware that there was anything to be repentant about. It was terribly unfair. She brooded, tossed and turned peevishly in the pink bedroom. She came through into the sitting room and sat on the side of the divan. She switched on the lamp, blinked in the harsh light, nudged her daughter awake.

"Ann dear, I'm worried about you."

"I'm all right," said Ann, moving restlessly on the cramped divan.

"Where did we go wrong?" puzzled Mrs. Walton. "We always taught you the difference between right and wrong."

"Yes, you did," Ann said. She sat upright, feeling the baby kicking and stretching.

"You were top in Scripture at school. Several times."

"Once," said Ann.

Mrs. Walton went back to her bed and lay down, unable to sleep. She propped herself up on the pillows. She heard a door open downstairs, the hoot of an owl, footsteps coming up the stairs. After a moment there was a faint swishing sound outside on the landing, like a cat rubbing itself along the carpet. Scratchings at the door. Fingernails on the glass. Mrs. Walton listened petrified. A low moaning began. "Let me in . . . let me in." The voice was weary, filled with pain.

Mrs. Walton got out of bed and stood behind the door with accelerated heart. She thought she could make out the shape of a man beyond the panel of the glass. Something at any rate. She went on all fours in her nylon nightdress across the sitting room. "Ann," she whispered urgently. "Ann."

Ann opened her eyes. She couldn't understand

what her mother was doing paddling about the room like a dog. She heard William calling: "Ann . . . Ann . . ."

"It's him," she said. "It's William." She wanted to jump up and let him in, but she didn't dare with her mother here. She knew William. He wouldn't be curtailed by the presence of her mother. The moaning went on.

"What's wrong with the fool?" hissed Mrs. Walton. "Does he think he's Heathcliff?" She had never known anything like it. Not even during the war when things were more casual.

She got in beside Ann on the divan. She kept tumbling out onto the carpet. They both began to giggle. Her mother smelt of powder and perspiration. The rings on her fingers snagged the blankets. It was like hiding from the enemy; outside in no-man's-land the wounded groaned, caught on the barbed wire.

In the morning, Ann refused to look on the landing.

"Don't be ridiculous," snapped her mother. "Go and see if he's still there."

"He won't be," Ann said mournfully.

Mrs. Walton was irritable with lack of sleep. She dressed and flounced into the kitchen to make breakfast.

"I can't stay much longer," she announced. "I must go home to Daddy. It's too noisy here."

Ann didn't want her mother to leave. After all it was too late now. William would never return. He had probably gone straight off to seek comfort from

Sheila or Edna or Pamela. He had let go of the branch forever. "Please stay," she begged. "Don't go yet."

"I don't know how you got involved with that person in the first place. He sounds absolutely insane. He needs putting away." Mrs. Walton slammed cups and saucers and marmalade jar onto the table. "Have you no pride?" she asked. It was torture to her, the thought of a weak indulgent man like that reducing her daughter to such straits. "No," said Ann. "I haven't."

"What does his wife say about his behaviour?"

"She says he's a beautiful person."

"Poor thing," said Mrs. Walton. "She needs her head examined. If a man treated me like that, going off with women, carrying on outside the door in the middle of the night, I wouldn't put up with it. I'd have him restrained." It was as if she was talking about a horse or a mad dog. Her chins quivered. "You talk about modern life and things being different now. You haven't learnt anything at all. All this permissiveness has led you young girls into slavery. I wouldn't give him house room."

"I want a cup of tea," said Ann. She was tired and she felt bulky and uncomfortable.

"There's no milk," said Mrs. Kershaw. "Go and see if there's any on the step."

"I can't," protested Ann.

Her mother crossed her arms and stamped her foot in fury. "I'm not drinking tea without milk," she cried.

Ann crept into the hall. No one. Not a sign. The

wardrobe was still there, the waiting pram. She looked for a letter on the mat. There was no milk in the porch.

As she crossed the hall to knock on Mrs. Kershaw's door, thinking she might borrow some, William leapt out of the wardrobe. He looked dreadful, dishevelled and white as chalk. His eyes glittered in his exhausted face. He seized her arm. He shook her brutally. "Why didn't you let me in, then?"

"I couldn't," she said, trembling with shock. "I couldn't."

"Has that bastard Gerald come back?"

She hesitated. She didn't want to mention her mother.

"I told that bastard to keep away. I told him I was going to marry you."

He let go of her. He began to run up the stairs.

"Wait," she cried, "Wait."

She caught up with him on the first landing. She hung onto his coat. "It's Mummy. It's my mother come to stay."

He sank onto the stairs. She sat beside him, stroking his hair.

"I thought I'd lost you," he said. They clung to each other.

"Come with me now," he said. "Come out with me. I want to take you away from here. It's all spoilt here."

"I can't," she whispered. "I can't leave my mother." She could have bitten her tongue.

William said, "I won't make any more promises. I won't say I'll do this or that. Just let's spend the day together."

She thought if she told her mother she was going to the hospital she could possibly stay out all morning. She might even say she fainted having her blood pressure taken and was put to bed for the afternoon.

"You've got so big," he said. "You're so full of baby." He spread his hands on her stomach.

"I could meet you in about an hour," she said. "I could meet you somewhere."

"At the little station on Finchley Road," he said. "We'll go to Hampstead Heath. We'll have a picnic."

*

It was warm on the Heath. The grass smelled of summer. He laid his coat on the ground for her to lie on. He had bought cornish pasties and fruit, a bottle of H.P. sauce. He wanted to know if he should buy her lemonade.

"No," she said. "I don't want any lemonade."

He didn't make any promises. She was disappointed. But he wanted her to make him one.

"What sort of a promise?" she asked.

"No matter what happens," he said. "No matter how I upset you, I have to be there when the baby's born."

"Will the hospital let you?" she asked. "Will they let you be there?"

"You're not to have it in the hospital," he said. "You're to have it at home, in that pink room where we began. When it wasn't spoilt. Do you understand?"

"Oh yes," she said. "I do understand."

She looked down at the grass so that he wouldn't see the tears in her eyes. She tried to reach back to the time when it was lovely, when it wasn't spoiled. She failed. He could do it, she knew. He was bigger than she in every way. She was petty and cynical.

"I don't think you're allowed to have your first child at home," she said. "In case there are complications."

"Rubbish. You're healthy . . . you're in the pink. They can't make you go into hospital."

She wondered if all the right things would be available—the drugs, the gas and air. What about blood poisoning. Puerperal fever?

"I promise," she said. "I'll have it at home." Even if it killed her, she would do as he asked.

There was little conversation between them. One topic would only lead to another. What have you been doing? Who with? It wasn't worth the risk. They lay in the sunshine, William pale, Ann in the pink, thinking their own thoughts, munching apples.

She slept for a while. When she awoke William was squatting beneath a tree, digging a hole with a stick.

"What are you doing?" she asked.

"I'm burying a lock of your hair."

"My hair?" she said, startled. She hadn't remembered ever giving him a piece of her hair.

"When we're old," he said. "We'll come back here together, and look for it."

He was so romantic . . . so beautiful.

The twig snapped in half. He laid a matchbox on

194

the ground. He felt in the grass for something else to poke out the earth. He stood up and wandered a little distance off, searching among the bushes and the stones.

She rolled over onto her large stomach and looked at the matchbox. An ant ran over her fingers. She shook it away and reached for the little carton with the coloured label. William turned and smiled at her. She smiled back. Birds sang. She opened the matchbox and looked at the lock of dark hair bound with white cotton.

She banged her face on the ground. She threw the twist of glossy hair at the tree. She ripped the matchbox into shreds with her teeth. Clumsily she rose to her feet, whirling round and round, crying out on a single piercing note.

William thought she had been stung by a wasp. He ran to her, trying to fasten her within his arms. She wrenched away from him and, continuing to scream, fled across the grass toward the pond. She thought if she ran fast enough she would dip down under the surface and be drowned instantly. The sunlight leapt upon the water; the quiet ducks, swimming in formation, squawked in alarm. By the time she was ankle deep in the pond she had changed her mind. It was too wet, too cold. She swerved sideways, stumbled up the bank, ran along the tree-lined path to the road. William caught her. She hit him in the face. He got her by a skein of hair and dragged her head backwards.

"Jesus," he cried. "What's wrong with you?"

She stared at him with hatred. She spat full into his face. She tore away from him with such violence that he was left with a hank of hair twined about his fist. He shook his fingers as if they were burnt, the yellow strands drifted downwards through the air and blew away among the grass.

"Bury that in a bloody matchbox," she screamed, running again, leaving him standing there in the sunshine.

7

Mrs. Walton went home after two weeks. Before she left, she told Ann the most searing stories about her own experience of childbirth: the pain, the torture in the bed, the doctor summoned three days early; the breaking of the waters, the labour, consultation downstairs between the doctor and Captain Walton.

"But what sort of pain?" persisted Ann, wanting to be prepared.

"Indescribable," said her mother. "The doctor said to my husband, "Choose between your wife and child. We can't save them both. Choose, man.""

"But why?" asked Ann. "What was wrong?"

"One of those things," Mrs. Walton said, spreading her hands out in ignorance. In the end only Mrs. Walton's teeth were lost. The baby was slapped hard on the buttocks and cried. The mother recovered.

"How awful," said Ann. It had certainly been an

uncomfortable experience for both of them.

"But it won't be like that for you," explained Mrs. Walton, a little late in the day.

She said she would knit something for the baby and send it through the post. She'd had a word with Mrs. Kershaw and as soon as Ann went into hospital, Mrs. Kershaw had promised to let her know. She hugged Ann.

"If that person comes again," she advised. "You call Roddy and tell him to phone the police."

"Yes," said Ann obediently. "I'll do that." She made her mouth tremble, her eyes glisten with tears. For her mother's sake.

"Cheer up," said Mrs. Walton, her own eyes filling.

Ann almost wished she might stay, but they both knew it would never last. Sooner or later one of them would say something to be regretted.

Down the stairs went the straw hat with the roses, out onto the path. A last wave of white glove as she stepped into the taxi.

She wrote a few days later, expressing disgust that Ann had landed her in such a predicament. She had told Mrs. Munro and Aimée Hughes that Ann had been married secretly for several months to a well-known writer. After all, Ann couldn't stay away indefinitely from Brighton. Captain Walton would be bound to ask questions, and some explanation had to be given for the baby. "Imagine my horror," she wrote, "when Mrs. Munro showed me the enclosed cutting. I don't know how I'm going to show my face at the Bridge Club."

There was a photograph of William and Edna

seated together. The article said William McClusky's play *The Truth is a Lie* was to open at Wyndham's
on August 3rd. It was to be adapted into a film and
he had been commissioned to write the screenplay.
Mr. and Mrs. McClusky were due to sail to the States
on the *Queen Elizabeth,* later in the year. Mrs.
McClusky said she was delighted. She had always
wanted to travel.

When Ann showed the cutting to Mrs. Kershaw
she said Roddy had already pointed it out to her.
She said, "I hoped you wouldn't see it."

"It's all right," said Ann. "I don't really mind."

She thought she was possibly anaesthetised by
the coming of the baby. Or punch drunk. Nothing
seemed to bother her anymore. Not love, certainly.
Only an insatiable curiosity to find out why, and
how, and with whom William lived his life. She
didn't want him to live with her at all. But she did
need to know who did. She telephoned Edna several times but there was never a reply.

William wrote her a letter, a week before the baby
was due. Did she remember her promise to him?
That day on the heath when the grass was warm and
golden. Green, she thought, pedantically. Grass was
never golden, only corn. It was typical of him to
recall the sunshine.

I must hold you to your promise, he said. It may be,
that my love for you, so destroyed by my liking for
compartments, will become whole and beautiful
again, when our child is born. If you will let me
come to you now, you will perhaps recognise, in my
care for you and our child, that I am indeed your

199

Sweet William, and not the monster you have made of me. Let me come. Let me bathe your face and hold your hand when the pain comes.

My play opens on Thursday. How I wish you could be there. Later there will be a film. We will go to America, you and I and our baby, and live in a house in California with oranges growing in the garden.

The only thing he omitted was his address.

"Leave it," said Mrs. Kershaw. "Don't have any more to do with him."

"Would there really be oranges in the garden?" asked Ann.

"Small ones," said Mrs. Kershaw. "Don't take any notice of him."

Ann had remembered her promise to William, even before he wrote the letter—even after that nightmare day in the Heath. She had told the hospital she wanted to have the baby at home—they had advised against it—but she was adamant. When the pains began she was to ring the Nurses' Home. She would have gas and air and pethadene. She must have a supply of newspapers ready and the room thoroughly cleaned. Any surplus furniture, apart from the bed, must be moved into another room.

A cradle had arrived, either from William or from Edna, made of wood. It was Swedish. Mrs. Kershaw gave her the newspapers. The bedroom looked bare and simple.

"Brace yourself," said Mrs. Kershaw, "to be shaved. That's the humiliating part."

Ann phoned Edna again. The baby was due on

August 1st. She was vast and distorted, belly swinging, skin stretched tight. She had heartburn for which she nibbled charcoal biscuits. Freckles appeared across the bridge of her nose.

"I've been away," said Edna. "Staying with my son."

"Will you tell William the baby is coming soon?"

"When?" asked Edna selflessly.

"Any day," said Ann. "He wants to be here to see it."

"I'll tell him," promised Edna.

"I never meant to upset you," Ann said. "At any rate you'll be going to the States with William. For his film."

Edna said, "My dear child, who can tell."

*

Ann got her first stab of pain when she was getting out of bed in the morning. It took her breath away.

"Aaahh," she cried. "Mummy."

When it had passed she went downstairs and knocked at Mrs. Kershaw's door. No reply. She went back upstairs to get the phone number of the nurse. She looked in her booklet supplied by the hospital. She watched the clock, waiting with beating heart for the next spasm to possess her. It was quite exciting. She looked at her teeth in the bathroom mirror, felt them one by one; they were firm and unblemished. She started down the stairs again, wondering if she should telephone her mother. On the second landing she was cut in half it seemed, by the vicious swipe of a knife. She began to pant, as they had

201

taught her at the hospital. If only she could reach the phone.

When she opened her eyes, it was to see William coming through the hall door. He lifted her up in his arms and carried her laboriously back upstairs. He laid her on the bed. He phoned the nurse.

"Guess what," he said. "Her name is Borman. Like Martin Bormann."

She didn't understand. "I want the gas and air," she said. "I want it now."

He laid his hand over her nose and mouth. He told her to breath in deeply. In . . . out . . . in . . . out . . . On his palm was the odour of cinnamon and french fern soap.

"It worked," she cried, as the pain loosed its grip and fell away.

He grew excited by his success. He massaged her back, her breast. He stood up and began to unbutton his trousers. The doorbell rang. It was Nurse Borman with her blessed apparatus.

The sun blazed through the window, the dust spiralled from the pink rug. Nurse Borman read a detective story at the foot of the bed. William stroked Ann's hair back from her forehead. Whenever the pain began she slammed the rubber nozzle against her mouth and sucked in the gas with desperate haste. She sang "The Green Oak Tree."

"I love you," said William.

"You don't," said Ann. She smiled woozily at him, at his white face, his snub nose, bent over the double bed. She sang louder than ever. A thunderstorm started outside in the street. The rain came down.

"When will it come?" asked William.

"Never," said Nurse Borman. "Not until she let's go of that appliance."

There was a point, however, when she couldn't stop the baby coming, when she had to bear down. The nurse put away her book. William held Ann's hand and told her to push. She couldn't help it. She felt as if a carriage and pair were driving through her body; she tried to hold onto the reins of the galloping horse. Away it went, faster and faster. She split in two. "Aaaaahhh," she screamed. And there was the baby, blue on the cotton sheet, heavy against her thigh. It was a boy.

She was comfy and tidy. Clean sheets. Nurse Borman had borrowed Mrs. Kershaw's chicken casserole to bath the baby in.

"She's a vegetarian," muttered Ann. "She stews beans in that. Farty beans." And she giggled.

William was in the other room making tea. The Nurse laid the baby beside Ann in the bed, wrapped like an old man in his muffler; the white shawl bound him tightly. He looked like Gerald.

Ann slept.

Mrs. Kershaw and Roddy came up later to see her. Roddy touched the curled fingers of the baby and looked sad. Mrs. Kershaw wept and kissed Ann. "How lovely," she said, over and over. "You are a clever girl."

When Ann woke in the evening, Roddy and William were drinking whisky by the bed. They were smiling at each other. Mrs. Kershaw made Ann an omelette. The boy, dark and perfect, slept in his Swedish cradle.

Chuck von Schreiber arrived at eight o'clock. He carried a bunch of flowers. Edna had sent them. He called Ann "the little mother." He didn't look at the baby.

"Have you got that book in the car?" asked William.

"Aye," said Chuck. "Come down and get it."

After some moments William looked at the child, touched its frail head, excused himself.

"I'll be back in a moment," he said.

He went out with Chuck.

Ann dozed. Mrs. Kershaw and Roddy sat on either side of the bed, drinking whisky from cups. Ann heard dimly the sound of the car's engine, the acceleration up the hill. Time passed.

"Where is he?" she asked.

She didn't really want to know. Not at that moment. She was trying to remember the particular shade of the glossy clump of hair she had flung away on the Heath. There must be an answer somewhere. An identification. One had to know the relationship between people. The whole secret of life was there, if only she could be given the clues.

Mrs. Kershaw went to the window and looked down in the evening street.

"He's bloody well gone," she said.

The dark-haired baby, with the beaked nose, began to cry.